MONTANA RANGER RETURNS

BROTHERHOOD PROTECTORS BOOK #18

ELLE JAMES

TWISTED PAGE INC

MONTANA RANGER RETURNS

BROTHERHOOD PROTECTORS BOOK #18

New York Times & USA Today
Bestselling Author

ELLE JAMES

ISBN EBOOK: 978-1-62695-379-6

ISBN PRINT: 978-1-62695-380-2

*For my sister, Delilah Devlin, for always having time
for me when I need help brainstorming and editing.
You're amazing, and I love you so very much.*

*For my readers who make my dreams come true by
keeping me in the business I love dearly...WRITING!
Much love and happiness to you all. Thank you for
buying my books!*
Elle James

AUTHOR'S NOTE

Brotherhood PRotectors Series
Montana SEAL (#1)
Bride Protector SEAL (#2)
Montana D-Force (#3)
Cowboy D-Force (#4)
Montana Ranger (#5)
Montana Dog Soldier (#6)
Montana SEAL Daddy (#7)
Montana Ranger's Wedding Vow (#8)
Montana SEAL Undercover Daddy (#9)
Cape Cod SEAL Rescue (#10)
Montana SEAL Friendly Fire (#11)
Montana SEAL's Mail-Order Bride (#12)
SEAL Justice (#13)
Ranger Creed (#14)
Delta Force Rescue (#15)
Dog Days of Christmas (#16)
Montana Rescue (#17)
Montana Ranger Returns (#18)

Visit ellejames.com for titles and release dates
and join Elle James's Newsletter at
https://ellejames.com/contact/

PROLOGUE

FIN MCCLAIN CHECKED his gear for the hundredth time, adrenaline rocketing through his system as he awaited their cue to jump.

He wasn't afraid of hurling his body out of an airplane, having done it more than a hundred times. As an Airborne Ranger, parachuting out of a perfectly good plane was what he did.

He and his team didn't always walk into enemy territory, they also jumped in, usually behind enemy lines, much like the operation ahead of him.

Their mission: to drop into the middle of ISIS-held territory and find the young girls who had been taken from their school in a small Syrian village. ISIS had made no effort to hide what they'd done. They'd paraded the frightened girls in front of cameras, showing the world that they were in control and would inflict their ancient laws on the region's people, using the little girls as an example.

The media-loving brothers nicknamed Jihadi Jim and Jihadi Joe led the procession, shouting death to the infidels in English. *American* English.

Fin's blood burned at what those girls must be going through and at the hands of radicalized American punks. He'd joined the Army to fight for the country he loved and for people like those children and other innocents who couldn't defend themselves. He hated that he was fighting against his own countrymen. Traitors.

Even back home in Eagle Rock, Montana, he'd learned the hard way that the enemy came in all shapes, sizes and sexes. And they might be standing right next to you. Hell, you might be married to them.

His chest tightened.

Ben Nelson, the man beside him, elbowed him in the side and shouted over the roar of the airplane's engine, "I hope we run into the Syrian female fighters on this mission. I hear they're bad-ass."

Fin had heard about the band of Syrian women who'd taken matters into their own hands to defend themselves and their children. He was curious about them as well. Special Forces teams had worked alongside them and had only good things to say about them.

"Nothing makes me hotter than a woman who can handle a gun," Nelson said with a grin.

"As long as it's not pointed at you or someone you care about," Fin muttered.

"True," his friend sighed and then glanced up. "Man, I hear you're heading home for some R&R when we get back to the States."

Fin nodded. He hadn't wanted to go home, but his commander had insisted.

His CO had called him into the operations tent the day before, a frown denting his brow. "Your family went so far as to notify the Red Cross to get in touch with you." He'd stood staring straight into Fin's eyes.

Fin had met the man's gaze for as long as he could before guilt made him look away. "I'm not much on writing, sir."

"Five years is a long time to go without spending time with your family."

Not long enough. And he kept up with them through the media. It wasn't hard when his sister was none other than the mega movie star Sadie McClain.

Fin lifted his chin. "I don't have much to say." He'd failed Sadie. Big time.

"Why didn't you tell us your sister is *the* Sadie McClain?" His commander had grinned. "She's an amazing actress."

And beautiful, kind and happy...now that he and his wife were out of the picture.

Ex-wife.

The crazy bitch had nearly succeeded in killing Sadie out of jealousy and greed.

The sad thing was that Fin hadn't clued in on her devious plan. He hadn't been able to comprehend or conceive of the idea that his high school sweetheart, whom he'd married soon after graduating, had that kind of evil in her or would direct her maleficence toward Fin's sister, Sadie.

Had it not been for Hank Patterson, Sadie would be dead. She wouldn't have married the love of her life, nor would she have had two beautiful, healthy children.

His niece, Emma, and nephew, McClain.

Fin had been an idiot to have trusted his wife, never believing she was capable of murder.

Thankfully, Hank had been there to protect Sadie. When Carla had gone to jail, Fin had hired a lawyer and ended their marriage. He'd apologized profusely to his sweet sister, but the damage had been done.

As a brother, he'd failed her.

He couldn't stay at White Oak Ranch, and he couldn't be around Sadie or her husband, knowing he had been sleeping with the enemy all along.

Sadie had been quick to lay the blame all at Carla's feet. But Fin should have seen what was going on and done everything in his power to protect his sister.

"Always wanted to go to Montana," Nelson yelled above the noise of the rotor whipping the air. His words brought Fin back to the present.

Fin would gladly let his Army buddy take his place. After five years, Fin still wasn't sure how to face his sister. He still felt as guilty about the attempts on her life as if he'd committed them himself.

The Army had given him an escape. A chance to do some good to make up for what his ex-wife had nearly accomplished. Sure, he'd like to get to know his niece, Emma, and his nephew, McClain Patterson. The boy would be almost a year old now.

He smiled at the name his sister and her husband had called their son—McClain Patterson, using Sadie's maiden name as the child's first name.

"Everybody up!" the team leader yelled.

Fin lurched to his feet, the bulk of his parachute weighing him down, reminding him of where his head should be.

Not in Montana, but in the moment, in the back of a C-130, about to jump into the hot zone where ISIS had taken the schoolgirls.

Wiping the past from his mind, he lined up with the others and shuffled toward the exit.

One by one, the Rangers stepped out of the airplane, plummeting toward the earth.

When it was Fin's turn, that rush of adrenaline shot fire through his veins. He stepped out and immediately dropped.

Already, the canopies of the soldiers who'd gone ahead of him were popping open. He pulled the ripcord, and his parachute unfurled. As the folds of fabric billowed open and caught the wind, his body was yanked upward.

He held onto the control lines and guided himself toward the designated landing zone a mile away from where the Intel guys had indicated the girls were being held. They land on the opposite side of the ridge from the encampment, retaining their element of surprise.

The darkness of night helped conceal their approach—as long as ISIS soldiers weren't looking up.

As he slowly drifted toward the ground, Fin

studied the compound they'd make their way toward once they were boots on the ground.

A small, isolated village clung to the side of a hill. Mud buildings blended with the land. Some had been destroyed when strafed by mortars fired by ISIS fighters. Others remained intact, giving the terrorists a place to lay low with their captives.

"We've got movement," Nelson's voice sounded in Fin's ear. "Vehicles are leaving the target."

A couple of dark SUVs pulled away from the village, heading north, lights out.

"Let's hope they don't contain the girls," Fin said.

"There are more captives than they'd have room for," Nelson said.

"Got a line of trucks approaching from the south," Sergeant Foster cut in. "Looks like people in the truck beds. And they're carrying weapons."

"Damn," Nelson said.

Fin's thoughts echoed Nelson's curse. They were only a ten-man team. Intelligence sources had estimated approximately one dozen ISIS soldiers guarding the girls. If they were getting reinforcements, the Rangers could be outnumbered two to one, or worse.

Some of the guys were hitting the ground when the sound of gunfire erupted from below Fin.

The trucks full of armed men had come to a halt short of the small village. The people in the back leaped out and ran toward the village, firing as they went.

The ground seemed to rush up at Fin. The ridgeline cut off his view of the village and muffled the sounds of gunfire.

When his feet touched the dirt, he tucked and rolled, absorbing the impact. As soon as he was completely down, he rolled to his feet and quickly unbuckled the harness, letting the canopy float away in the wind.

The team gathered briefly, accounted for everyone, and then headed up the hillside to the top of the ridge.

Once there, they paused and took in what was happening below.

The gunmen who'd unloaded from the pickups were pinned down just outside the village walls by a machine gun nest perched on the corner of one of the remaining buildings that hadn't been destroyed.

"Dude," Nelson said. "Those aren't dudes."

Fin looked away from the machine gunner and focused on the people lying flat on the ground. Even in the dark, with only the light from the stars above, he could tell they were smaller than most men and...curvier. At one point, long, dark hair blew up around the head of one of the figures lying against the ground whose weapon was trained on the village walls.

"I think you're going to get your wish, Nelson," Fin said. "Those are female fighters, and they're gunning for whoever is inside those walls."

"Hopefully, the schoolgirls are staying safe and low," Sergeant Foster said. "Looks like they could use some help." He turned to Fin. "Think you can get a bead on the gunner?"

Fin aimed his rifle at the top of the building and peered through his scope. A brick wall stood between the Rangers and the gunner, making it impossible for him to target the man who was firing down at the female fighters.

"No can do. I'd have to come at him from a different angle. Got a wall in the way."

"And we can't fire up the grenade launcher at him," Sergeant Foster said, his voice grim. "We don't know where the girls are located."

"Then we'll have to take him out the hard way," Fin said.

The sergeant nodded. "Let's do this."

Fin and the team of Rangers slipped over the ridgeline and descended the hillside, moving toward the village. At first, the gunner on top of the building didn't see them.

They'd made it to the bottom and were just starting across the open space between the hillside and the closest building when the gunner turned his weapon on the Rangers.

"Take cover!" Foster shouted. "Nelson, McClain, on my mark…"

Having taken cover behind a boulder, Fin bunched his muscles and awaited the command to take point. He and Nelson would breach the wall, get to the top of the building and take out the gunner.

In a brief break in the barrage of bullets being expelled from the machine gun, an engine revved loudly from behind the line of female fighters.

"What the hell?" Foster muttered into the radio.

Out of the dark shadows behind the female soldiers burst a lone figure on a motorcycle, racing toward the village entrance. The helmeted driver maneuvered the bike with one hand while he aimed a rifle toward the top of the building.

For a moment, Fin froze, transfixed by the balls of the rider charging into certain death.

"Go!" Foster shouted.

The order shook Fin into action. He leaped to his feet and ran the few yards in the open.

The gunslinging motorcycle rider raced in from a different direction, zigzagging to minimize himself as a target. The machine gunner had to choose whom to aim for.

Fortunately for Fin and Nelson, he chose the faster threat...the rider on the motorcycle.

Fin reached the wall first, bent and cupped his hands.

Nelson arrived seconds later, stepped into Fin's hands and launched himself up onto the wall.

The gunner continued to fire on the advancing motorcycle rider, missing his mark.

Fin couldn't help but watch as the rider continued to zigzag until he came within a few feet of the opening of the wall into the village. By then, he was too close for the gunner to get a clear shot.

The cyclist slid sideways, the bike laying over on its side, coming to a halt with its wheels up against the wall.

Fin's breath caught and held, praying the rider would get up.

When he didn't, Fin's heart beat faster.

Sergeant Foster arrived at the wall along with four other men. "We'll cover for Nelson." The sergeant lifted his chin toward the downed motorcycle rider. "See what you can do to save him. The others will provide cover for you should other bogeys come out to play."

The machine gunner aimed toward the female fighters again, raining bullets down on them, holding them in place.

Foster and three other men went over the wall, leaving Fin to accomplish his orders.

After a glance toward the female fighters, he had to hope they wouldn't fire on him, thinking he was one of the bad guys.

He ran along the base of the village wall toward the downed motorcycle rider.

When he reached the bike, the sound of shouts and running footsteps gave him a sense of urgency.

Fin reached down to feel for a pulse.

Before he could touch his fingers to the rider's neck, a slender hand grabbed his wrist. "I'm fine, but you'll be dead if you don't get out of here now."

The voice was firm—and decidedly feminine.

The figure lying on the ground, dressed in black leather pants and a black jacket, tried to pull her leg from beneath the bike.

Fin lifted it enough for her to free her calf. "Can you stand?"

"I think so." She rolled to her side and pushed to her knees, facing the village. Suddenly, she shouted, "Get down!"

A man dressed all in black, wearing a black mask over his face, stepped out from the walled village, turned his rifle on the woman and fired.

The bullet hit the ground beside the man's target, missing her and Fin.

The motorcycle rider dropped to one knee, pulled a handgun from beneath her jacket and fired before the man could pull the trigger again. He dropped where he stood, unmoving.

More footsteps pounded on the ground on the other side of the wall and shouts filled the air.

"Let's go." Fin helped her to her feet then took her hand and turned to run.

She dug in her heels and shook her head. "Not fast enough." She pulled free of his grip and tried to lift the motorcycle onto its wheels. She struggled, the bike falling back to the ground.

Fin stood the bike on its wheels and slung his leg over the seat. "Get on," he shouted.

She slipped on behind him, wrapped her arms around his waist and held on as he kickstarted the bike, revved the throttle and took off, driving along the base of the wall away from the gunner. Then he took off across the open field.

He didn't slow until they were well away from the village, dodging boulders from the hillside. When he thought they were out of gunfire range, he pulled the bike behind a boulder and killed the engine.

The woman slid off the back, unbuckled her helmet and lifted it over her head, dropping it to the ground. Long dark hair fell around her shoulders. She spun back toward the fight they'd left behind. "Why did you take me so far away? I need to be there…to help."

Fin was shocked that she spoke English with an American accent.

"Are you American?" he asked.

She didn't answer. Instead, she stepped out from behind the boulder, heading back into the fight. After she'd taken only two steps, she swayed, her knees buckling.

Fin reached out, slipped an arm around her waist and held her until her legs steadied beneath her. "You can't go back. Not now."

"I have to. They need help."

He held up a finger as voices sounded in his headset.

"Going in," Nelson said.

Moments later, the machine gunfire ceased.

A cheer went up from the female fighters as they rose to their feet and headed toward the opening in the wall around the village.

At that moment, half a dozen men carrying rifles emerged.

The woman in Fin's arms gasped.

Gunfire erupted.

The female fighters dropped to the ground and returned fire.

Between the Rangers and the female fighters, the ISIS rebels didn't stand a chance. Four went down. Two ducked back into the village.

More gunfire sounded from within the walls.

Several minutes later, Nelson's voice came across Fin's headset. "Found them."

"The girls?" Fin asked.

"Yes. They're scared but appear to be unharmed."

"Stand guard," Sergeant Foster said, "while we clear the area."

The remaining Rangers moved into the village.

Minutes later, Foster's voice sounded in Fin's ear. "All clear. Transport's on the way."

Fin stared into the woman's dark eyes, noting high cheekbones and a straight, perfect nose. "It's over. They found the schoolgirls."

She drew in a deep breath and let it out slowly, nodding her head. "Thank you, soldier," she murmured. Then she stared up into his eyes. "I have to go."

He shook his head and held on, refusing to release her. "You can barely stand."

"I'll be okay." She cupped his cheeks in her palms, leaned up on her toes and pressed a kiss to his lips. Then she stepped free of his arms, scooped up her helmet, slipped it over her head, buckled the strap beneath her chin and climbed onto the bike. With a quick nod, she drove away into the darkness.

Fin's gaze followed her until she disappeared out of sight.

He rejoined his team inside the village wall, where a dozen of little girls huddled close together.

The female fighters had joined the Rangers, taking over guard duty of the girls, holding them when they cried and murmuring soothing words in their language.

Sergeant Foster spotted Fin, a frown pulling his eyebrows together. "What happened to the guy on the motorcycle?"

"The guy was a girl." Fin's lips quirked upward on the corners as he recalled the soft warmth of her lips on his. "She left."

"She left?" Foster's frown deepened. "I thought he...she...was with the female fighters. Did you at least get her name?"

Fin shrugged. "She left before I could. By her accent, I would guess she's American or Canadian."

"I don't care if she's Martian," Foster said. "I'd like to know who it was that distracted the gunner so that we could get inside and stop him. She saved our asses."

"What she did could have been suicide," Fin said. "She sacrificed herself so that we could get inside." He wished he'd stopped her from leaving. "Surely, one of the female fighters knows who she is." He looked around for someone to ask.

The leader of the female-led Syrian soldiers stepped forward and spoke in halting English. "She is an Angel…" Her brow twisted as she seemed to search for words. "To ISIS, she is Angel…of Death." Her chin rose. "To us…Angel of Freedom."

"You don't know her name?" Fin asked.

The leader shook her head. "She appears in our time of need…then she is gone."

She'd done the same for the Rangers, risking her own life to take the focus off the Rangers and place it on her.

Foster held out one of the rifles he'd confiscated off a dead ISIS terrorist. "Did you see this?

Fin shook his head.

Foster shined a small flashlight down on the rifle. "This weapon was manufactured in the US."

Fin frowned. "So?"

"How did it get into the hands of these guys?"

"Sometimes, I feel like we're fighting a war against our own countrymen."

"We found several empty wooden crates in one of the buildings. We think they were once full of these shiny new rifles."

"Do you think they were trading the girls for weapons?"

"I wouldn't put it past them. What better way to fund their cause?" With a sigh, Fin glanced in the direction his angel had gone. He could still feel the warmth of her lips on his and could kick himself for not holding onto her long enough to learn her name.

He doubted he'd ever know.

His team was due to return to the States within the next week. He didn't know when or if he'd ever return to Syria. If he did come back, the chances of finding her were slim.

CHAPTER 1

THREE WEEKS LATER...

AFTER LEAVING BUTTE, Montana, she followed Interstate highway 90, heading east, winding through Beaverhead-Deerlodge National Forest.

Her eyelids grew heavy as she passed the Continental Divide, and she focused on the road ahead, letting the chill mountain air wash over her. Thankfully, she wore a sheepskin-lined leather jacket and gloves. However, her hands were cramping from holding onto the handlebars of the motorcycle. She only had to hold on for a little more than an hour more to reach her destination.

She had to get there. The sooner, the better.

After what had happened to her father, she couldn't be too late to save her last living relative.

Headlights blinked in her tiny rearview mirror. As late as it was, she'd expected to be the only one on the road besides truck drivers moving cargo across the country.

She'd left Coeur d'Alene as soon as she'd gotten home and discovered the house empty. Immediately hitting the road for Bozeman, Montana, she'd called but had gotten no answer.

Several times along the five-hour ride, she'd called…again, no response.

God, please, don't let me be too late.

She'd broken every speed limit, slowing only slightly as she'd passed major towns along the way and stopping in Butte for gas.

It was after she'd left Butte that she'd realized the headlights in her rearview mirror were keeping pace with her. Not closing the distance nor overtaking her to pass on the long, lonely stretch of road.

It could be someone following her to let her smoke out any state troopers looking to dish out a speeding ticket. Or it could be whoever had followed her from her home through the streets of Coeur d'Alene. She thought she'd shaken her tail before she'd hit the interstate heading east to Bozeman.

It didn't make sense for anyone to follow her for hours down the highway unless they wanted to get to where she was going.

Or maybe her sleep-deprived brain was reading too much into the bright lights, blinding her every time she glanced back.

Yet, she'd been looking over her shoulder ever since she'd left the embassy twenty-nine hours ago. After her father's assassination, she'd had no reason to stay. Hell, she couldn't stay, even if she'd wanted. Her father's service there ended with his life. She'd been living with him.

She did not belong there, didn't have a work visa and couldn't continue to live in the country. Her self-imposed tour of duty had come to an end. The note found in her father's car with the bodies of her father and his driver had been clear. The identity of the Angel of Death had been discovered. The ISIS leader, Abu al-Jarbah, wanted revenge for the loss of his brother Abu Sahayb in the latest skirmish that had cost nineteen ISIS terrorists. They wouldn't stop until they'd killed her and all her family.

Leaving the disposition of her father's body to the embassy, she'd flown back to the States on the carliest flight she could find. Sleep had escaped her. Even on the plane, she'd kept her eyes open and had watched for any movement from other passengers. An ISIS fighter could make his move on a crowded plane, unafraid of killing everyone on board.

Thankfully, nothing had happened on the plane. Still, she hadn't slept in two days.

Her focus turned to the highway ahead. One more hour and she'd be at her destination. One more hour to protect the only family she had left in the world. One more hour and she'd find a place to hide and sleep.

Her hands holding tightly to the handlebar, she yawned.

Lights glared in the rearview mirror. She glanced up, her eyes blinded by headlights.

The vehicle that had maintained a half-mile distance behind her for so long had increased its speed, catching up to her in a few short seconds.

Slow to react, she'd barely sped up when the car behind her slammed into the back of her bike, sending her skidding to her right toward the guardrails.

She twisted her handlebar to the left, fishtailing across the pavement, unable to correct her course.

With no control over her motorcycle, she slid toward the guardrail.

The front wheel of the bike caught the metal railing and flipped, throwing her over the top.

She tumbled down a steep embankment. The motorcycle bounced, rolled and slid down the hill, nearly hitting her several times before flying over the edge of a cliff.

Knowing she would be next if she didn't stop her descent, she reached out for anything to grab hold of as she somersaulted, rolled and slid down the hillside toward certain death. At one point, her helmet hit a boulder so hard the strap slipped out from under her chin, and the helmet flew off.

At the same time, her hands clasped a root sticking out of the ground. She held on, even as her momentum kept her flying down the hillside. When her body passed her hands holding the root, she jerked abruptly, her fingers losing their grip on the root.

Her headlong plunge slowed and came to a complete stop when her head bounced against a boulder.

A flash of pain ripped through her temple, mixing with the residual lights from being blinded by headlights. Then her world went blessedly black as she dove into blessed unconsciousness.

. . .

THE ELEVEN-HOUR DRIVE from Joint Base Lewis-McChord was long and tedious. Just what Fin had hoped it would be. Flying would've gotten him home quicker, but he really didn't want to get there any sooner than he had to.

If his commander hadn't ordered him home, he wouldn't have gone. Throughout the long drive, he'd gone over and over in his mind what he would say to his sister. All he could come up with was, "I'm sorry."

It wasn't enough. His wife had nearly killed Sadie. The woman was crazy jealous of Sadie's success and that she was half-owner of the White Oak Ranch.

Carla, his high school sweetheart and wife of six years, had gone on a secret rampage to kill Sadie McClain, the movie star and Fin's only sister.

If Sadie had died, Fin and Carla would've owned all of White Oak Ranch. Carla had revealed that she would have killed Fin to become the sole owner of the property worth so much more now, with celebrities purchasing large tracts of land in the state for vacation homes away from the crowds in LA.

Carla's duplicity and evil intentions had

stunned Fin. He couldn't have conceived of someone with so much hatred in her soul. Much less someone he'd married. He no longer trusted his character judgment. Nor did he trust any other woman besides his sister, Sadie, who had a heart of gold without a single malevolent bone in her body.

He'd passed Butte and was well on his way toward Bozeman when he spotted movement on the side of the steering wheel to the left, he swerved to miss what at first he thought was a deer stepping out into the road. It wasn't until a woman stumbled out onto the pavement that he realized it wasn't a deer. She fell to her knees and then sank to a prone position on the highway.

Fin slammed on his brakes, bringing his truck to a skidding halt, inches away from the body lying on the pavement.

He tapped the hazard lights button, shifted into Park and dropped down out of the truck. He wasn't sure how busy the highway was in the early hours of the morning. If he didn't get her out of the way, the woman might lie there until she was run over by oncoming traffic.

He couldn't let that happen.

Since they were in the middle of a national forest, the woman had to have been involved in an accident. There was no other reason for her to be out on that highway this late at night by herself.

In the bright beams of his pickup's headlights, Fin knelt beside her and felt the base of her throat, searching for a pulse. She had a long streak of blood running from her temple down to her chin. Her black leather jacket and pants were torn and dirty, and her dark hair hung in tangled disarray around her face and shoulders.

When the thump of a strong pulse beat beneath his fingertips, he let go of the breath he'd been holding and frowned down at the unconscious woman.

He'd been trained in battlefield first-aid. Normally, he wouldn't move an accident victim until an EMT arrived. Moving them could cause further injuries. But he couldn't leave her in the middle of the road, and the last time he'd glanced at his cellphone, he'd had no service. The only way to get her to a hospital was to take her there himself. Calling for an ambulance wasn't an option.

He slipped his arms beneath her knees and shoulders and lifted her.

She moaned, but her eyes remained closed.

The hair in her face slipped back, revealing high cheekbones, dark eyebrows and a straight, perfect nose. Beneath the blood drying on her face, she was a beauty.

And very familiar to Fin. He just couldn't put his finger on why. Not yet. But he would, once he got her to a hospital.

Fin wasn't sure what had happened to her. He didn't see a crashed vehicle anywhere, and he didn't have time to go looking for it. The most important thing was to seek medical attention.

"Come on, let's get you to a hospital," he murmured.

Again, she moaned, and her eyes fluttered open, then immediately closed.

Fin could swear she'd said no.

"You've been injured," he said as he strode toward his truck, managed to get the back passenger side door open, and laid her on the back seat. Still, she didn't wake up, which worried him.

He buckled her in and then climbed into the driver's seat and headed for Bozeman. When he got there, he'd hand her over to the hospital and be on his way to his sister's house.

Hell, he might stay the rest of the night at a hotel in Bozeman. He hated to keep his sister and her husband awake for so long.

Truthfully, he wanted to delay his little family reunion as long as possible. Finding the woman in the middle of the road and getting her to a medical facility took precedence, giving him as good an excuse as any.

Once the woman was safely in the hands of the ER staff at the hospital in Bozeman, he'd find a hotel and finish the rest of his journey in the morning. Maybe by then, he'd have come up with the words he needed to say to his sister and her husband, expressing his deepest regrets and apologies for what they'd gone through because he hadn't seen through his wife's machinations.

Half an hour into the drive into Bozeman, the woman in the back seat pushed to a sitting position and stared at him in the rearview mirror.

Her eyes narrowed, and she pressed a hand to the side of her head, wincing. "Who are you, and where are you taking me?"

"I'm Fin McClain," he responded. "I'm taking you to the hospital."

She shook her head and winced again. "No. Can't."

He frowned. "Can't what?"

"Can't take me..." she closed her eyes and pinched the bridge of her nose, "hospital. They can't find me."

"Who can't find you?" Fin asked, his gaze alternating between the road in front of him and the woman swaying in the backseat of his pickup.

She continued to pinch the bridge of her nose for another moment and then glanced up, her eyes wide and frightened. "I don't know. I just know they can't find me."

Fin's lips twisted. "That doesn't help. Maybe if I knew your name, I could help you figure it out…?" He cocked an eyebrow as he glanced in the mirror, meeting her gaze.

She shook her head, her brow furrowing. Then she squeezed her eyes shut as if trying to work something out. When she opened them, they were shining with unshed tears. "I don't know my name." Her hand rose to the side of her head where the streak of blood originated. "What happened?"

"I'm not sure," Fin said. "You staggered out onto the road in front of me and passed out. I assumed you were in some kind of accident. Since there's no cellphone reception out here to call for an ambulance, I had no choice but to take you to the hospital myself."

"I don't want to go to the hospital. I don't have time," she said, looking around as if for the answers to a hundred questions. Her gaze met his in the rearview mirror. "Where exactly are we?"

That was a question he could answer for her. "We're about thirty miles west of Bozeman."

"Montana?"

He laughed. "That's the only Bozeman I know of." His smile faded at the fear in her eyes.

"I know Bozeman is in Montana…." She cupped her cheeks and stared at the back of Fin's seat. "But I don't know my name. How can that be?"

"You've had a head injury. I've seen guys suffer head trauma in battle and have temporary amnesia. Maybe that's what's happened to you."

"Did they eventually remember?" she asked, staring hard into his reflected eyes.

"The guys I knew personally did recover their memories. Within a few days."

"I don't have a few days," she murmured. "I don't have time to forget."

"Why?" he asked.

She tipped her head back and moaned. "I don't know why. I just *know*." The woman rocked in her seat. "I have to get somewhere." She gripped her head in her hands. "It's urgent that I do. But where?"

"I can't help you with that. All I can do is get you to medical care. Maybe they can help you."

She nodded and looked into his eyes again. "Thank you, soldier."

The dark eyes, thick dark hair and the way she spoke those words blasted through his memories like a bullet from the barrel of a rifle.

He knew he'd seen her before. Her face and voice had sparked the recollection, but he hadn't been able to place her because she wasn't in the place he had seen her before.

The name *Angel* came immediately to mind, and with it, a storm of images in a star-studded sky over Syria.

His breath caught in his throat, and his heart pounded inside his chest. This woman was the Angel of Death. The woman on the motorcycle who had sacrificed her safety to draw the attention of a machine gunner away from a team of Rangers and the Syrian female fighters long enough for the Rangers to neutralize the gunner.

He looked in the mirror again, studying her face. Surely, it wasn't her. The last time he'd seen her, she'd been on the other side of the world, riding away from him on a motorcycle. This couldn't be the same woman. Could it?

She frowned. "What?"

"Does the name Angel mean anything to you?" he asked.

She tipped her head slightly to the side, her eyes narrowing as if contemplating the word. After a moment, she covered her face with her hands. "No. It means nothing."

"You don't remember anything about yourself?"

Her hands fell to her lap, and she stared out the side window. "Nothing. I don't even know if I have family looking for me. What if they're waiting for me to come home, worried that I haven't arrived?" She glanced down at her hands. "I'm not wearing a ring, so maybe I don't have a husband waiting at home."

"Do you know how old you are?"

She shook her head. "No."

"What state do you live in?"

Again, she shook her head. "No."

"Do you know what day it is?" he asked.

"No," she wailed and buried her face in her hands. "I don't remember anything."

"Do you remember my name?"

Her eyebrows pulled together. "Fin…McClain."

He nodded. "So, you can remember things since the accident, just nothing before."

"But why am I in Montana?" she asked. "Do I live here?"

"Sorry. I only just met you." His brow wrinkled. "Sort of. I still don't know your name. So, that makes two of us." He grinned to soften his words. "Hey, you're going to be okay. Let the docs look you over and make sure there isn't anything major wrong with you."

"But I can't. They'll find me."

"Who will find you?" he asked before he could catch himself.

"I don't—"

"—know," he finished for her. "Sorry. It has to be frustrating to have your memories wiped clean."

"It's terrifying," she whispered. "My whole life before now…is gone." Her words faded into the darkness.

The starkness in her gaze ripped at Fin's heart. "We're entering Bozeman now. Let's see what the docs say. Maybe after an X-ray or CT scan, they'll know more about what happened and why you're having trouble remembering."

He pulled into the drop-off zone of the emergency room at the main hospital in Bozeman. Thankfully, it was right off the interstate highway.

Fin was worried about the woman in the back seat of his truck. He didn't want to keep calling her *the woman*, but he didn't have her name.

He shifted into Park, got out and walked around to the passenger side of his truck to help her down. "We need to call you something when we check you in. Even if it's only temporary." He reached out to grip her around her waist.

"I don't know my name," she said, allowing him to lift her from her seat and lower her gently to the ground. Her knees buckled, and she would've fallen if he hadn't been holding onto her.

Her hand rested on his chest. "I feel like I should know you." She stared up into his eyes. "Do I?"

If she wasn't the Angel of Death from Syria, she could have been her doppelganger. Yet, Angel hadn't rung any bells with her. Then again, the leader of the Syrian female fighters had called her the Angel of Death. Perhaps, she hadn't heard that name associated with her. Or, like her given name, she'd forgotten it as well.

Since he wasn't sure of his memory of the Angel of Death, whom he'd only known for the space of less than half an hour in the middle of a hot combat zone, he could be wrong. God forbid, he told her she was the Angel of Death only to find out he'd been way off base. That might scare her even more. Her name would have to be Jane.

CHAPTER 2

WHEN JANE'S legs were steady beneath her, Fin slipped an arm around her waist and guided her through the automatic sliding glass doors and up to the reception desk.

"Name, please," the receptionist asked, her gaze on the computer screen in front of her.

Fin didn't answer for her, hoping the receptionist's curt request would jog her memory.

"I don't know," Jane replied.

The lady shot a glance toward her, a frown creasing her brow. "You don't...." She shook her head. "Reason for your visit?"

Fin felt Jane's body shake as she snorted. "I don't know." She squeezed her eyes shut tightly. "That's the problem. No matter how hard I try, I can't remember anything before this man found me on the highway." Opening her eyes, she stared at the lady behind the desk. "I don't know my name, where I'm from, or even how old I am. Make it up. It's as good as I would be able to do."

The receptionist tapped the keyboard with all her fingers without actually keying anything. "We have to enter a name."

"For God's sake," Fin bit out. "Jane Doe. Can we get on with it? She's been in an accident. We don't know what other damage has been done besides the memory lapse. She needs to see a doctor."

The receptionist glared at Fin for a second and opened her mouth to retort. Instead, she shut it and smiled, batting her eyelashes. "Of course. Thankfully, it's a slow night. You shouldn't have to wait long." She entered the name in the system. "You can have a seat until your name is called."

Fin helped Jane to a seat.

Once she had lowered herself onto the cushion, he backed away. "Do you need me, or are you good on your own?"

She shot a frightened glance his way. "You're leaving me?"

That had been his plan from the beginning. He realized she had to be scared when he thought about what she was going through, not knowing who she was or anything about her past. He was the only person she knew, and that was only because he'd found her and driven her into Bozeman. Still, he was probably her lifeline.

"I need to park the truck. It's blocking the drop-off point." He drew in a deep breath and committed. "I'll be right back."

Her chest rose and fell with a deep breath, and then she nodded. "Okay."

He turned and left her sitting in that chair in the near-empty lobby. As he reached the door, he glanced over his shoulder.

Jane's gaze was on him, desperate, hopeful, alone.

He couldn't just leave her. At least not until they admitted her and found a room for her in the hospital.

Hell, what if they released her? Where would she go? He refused to think that far ahead. He'd take one step at a time with Jane.

He was back in two minutes, hurrying through the automatic doors. He didn't know why he hurried. Had he expected her to disappear while he'd parked the vehicle?

As much as Jane wanted to know who she was, Fin did, too. If there was any chance she was the Angel of Death from the mission in Syria, he had to know for sure. And if she was, he had to know what had brought her to Montana and why she was sure someone would find her and possibly do her harm.

When he entered the lobby, his gaze went to the chair where he'd left Jane. She wasn't there. For a moment, his heart stopped, and he held his breath, his gaze searching the room for the dark-haired mystery woman.

"Over here," her voice called out.

He turned to find her sitting in a chair to his right, against the wall. Fin hurried to her side and dropped into the chair on her left.

"I had to move," she said. "There was a vent above me, blowing cold air on me." She shivered, rubbing her arms with her hands.

Fin frowned. He hadn't brought in his jacket and didn't want to go back out to retrieve it and leave her alone again. "If you want, I can put my arm around you. My body temperature usually runs hot."

"Please," she said quietly, leaning toward him.

He wrapped his arm around her back and pulled her against his side. "Better?"

Though she was stiff in his embrace, she nodded. "Much."

No sooner had she settled against him than a

nurse stepped out of a room and called out, "Jane Doe."

Fin chuckled. "So much for warming up."

"I'll be okay," she said. "As long as I keep moving."

Fin helped her to her feet and guided her to the small room, where she was asked to step onto a scale. When she stumbled, he was there to steady her and help her up onto the machine, and then he helped her back down when the nurse had the weight recorded.

Jane sat in a chair while the nurse took her temperature and blood pressure.

When she was done, she smiled gently. "I'm going to get you back to a room. Wait here while I get a wheelchair."

Jane frowned. "I can walk."

The nurse nodded. "I'm sure. But if it's all the same to you, I'd rather you didn't. When a head injury is involved, it's probably better to let me wheel you back. We don't want to risk you falling and injuring yourself more. I'll be right back."

The nurse left the room.

Jane leaned her head against the wall and closed her eyes, a shiver making her entire body shake.

"How are you holding up?" Fin asked.

Jane opened one eye. "I'd say I don't know, but I'm tired of saying it. I'd like to know everything I've forgotten. I feel so...so..." she raised her hand in the air, "...lost. Like I'm adrift in an awful nightmare. And I can't shake this sense of urgency. I need to get somewhere...I just don't know where that is."

Fin captured her hand and held onto it. "Give it time. You've been in an accident. Your body and mind are trying to recover. Maybe it's your system's way of protecting you."

"I'd rather it didn't protect me. I can take care of myself."

The nurse reappeared with the wheelchair.

Fin and the nurse helped Jane into it.

Once she was settled, the nurse faced Fin. "You can wait out in the lobby."

"I'd like him to come with me," Jane said, having reclaimed her hold on his hand. She glanced up at him, her eyes wide, pleading.

His chest tightened. Those dark eyes held him captive, and he found himself nodding.

The nurse's brow puckered. "Is he a relative?"

Jane shook her head. "I don't know."

"Only a relative can accompany you into the examination room," the nurse said.

Jane's lip curled upward. "He could be my fiancé for all I know."

The nurse's frown eased. "Fiancés count." She jerked her head toward the hallway in front of Jane and the wheelchair. "Follow me."

Fin had only meant to drop Jane Doe at the hospital and leave. He had no additional responsibility for the woman, and the medical staff would take care of her. But he found himself following the nurse down the hallway and into one of the examination rooms.

He helped Jane out of the wheelchair and onto the gurney.

The nurse adjusted the bed so that Jane was reclining, not lying flat on her back. She fluffed a thin pillow behind her. "Is that okay?"

Jane nodded. "Thank you."

"Could you get her a blanket?" Fin asked.

"Of course." The nurse exited the room and returned with a blanket that had been warmed.

Fin helped her drape it across Jane's body.

Jane caught his hand and held on while the nurse cleaned the wound on her temple, gently dabbing at the crusted blood until she'd wiped it away, leaving Jane's cheek clean.

"The doctor will be with you shortly." With

that, the nurse left the room, pulling the door closed slightly.

Alone, Fin stared down at where their hands were clasped, at a loss for words. He couldn't ask her anything about herself, like the usual getting-to-know-you kind of conversation. It would all be one-sided about him as long as Jane couldn't remember her past.

Her fingers were long and slender, and her grip firm. He liked the way her hand fit inside his.

Now that he had her in a brightly lit room, he studied her from head to toe, his gaze pausing on the tears in her leather jacket and pants. The garments were ruined, but they'd served their purpose. Jackets and pants could be replaced. Her skin and body would've been a bigger mess had she not been wearing the thick leather.

"I'd like to talk," Jane said softly. "But I can't remember anything to talk about." She grimaced up at him. "What about sports?"

Fin chuckled. "What about them?"

"Do you have a favorite sport or team?"

He nodded. "Football and the Seattle Seahawks."

"Are you from Seattle?"

Fin shook his head.

She tilted her head to one side. "You don't

strike me as someone who would enjoy living in a big city."

"I don't enjoy it. I prefer wide-open spaces where you can see for miles and miles."

"Like across a prairie or like being perched on a mountainside?" Jane asked.

"Both. I like the beauty of both places. I just don't enjoy the hustle and hassle of traffic and millions of people in one area."

Jane nodded. "Me either." Her eyes widened. "I don't like crowds."

Fin smiled. "See? It'll come back."

Her shoulders slumped. "Sooner would be better than later. I don't like being nameless and confused." She lay back against the pillow and closed her eyes.

"Tell me more about you," she said.

"Like what?"

"You like the Seahawks. What else?" She turned her head toward him and opened her eyes. "Since I don't know anything about me, maybe something about you will jog my memories."

"I grew up in Montana," he said. "I like to ride horses, hunt and fish." Fin shrugged.

"What about family?" She frowned. "I didn't think to ask... Are you married?"

Fin stiffened. That was the last question he

wanted to answer. It opened up too big a can of stinking worms.

JANE COULD SENSE she'd struck a nerve. The man was married, and she's been clinging to him like he was single and free to be with her for hours on end. "Hell, I'm so sorry. I've kept you from getting home." She let go of his hand as if it were too hot to hold. "You don't have to stay with me. I'm fine. Really."

Though she'd said she was fine, she was anything but fine. If and when Fin left, she'd be alone with nowhere to go and no one she knew. She didn't have any identification on her and no money or credit cards.

"I can manage on my own."

Fin drew in a deep breath and let it out. He even pinned a tight smile on his face. "No, I'm staying until I know you're going to be okay."

"I'm okay," Jane insisted. "I have a little headache and can't remember shit, but all my bones are where they should be. I could get up and walk right out of here if I wanted." She sat up fast as if to do just that. However, her head swam, and her vision blurred.

Fin was there to catch her before she slid over

the side of the gurney. "Hey, slugger, give yourself a break, will ya? Let the doc check you out and make sure you haven't got any swelling or bleeding that can be associated with head injuries."

His hand on her back was warm and strong as he eased her back against the pillow. "You didn't answer my question," she pointed out. Still curious, even though she'd told him, he didn't have to tell her. "Is she going to be mad when you don't show up on time?"

Fin shook his head. "No. I'm not married." His lips thinned into a flat line.

There was more to his simple statement than he was willing to give freely. "Were you?" she asked.

He looked away. "I was."

"I'm sorry."

"For what?" he asked, his voice harsh.

"For your loss…?" Jane guessed.

He frowned. "Oh, she's not dead."

"Divorce?"

He nodded. No details, which Jane found a little frustrating. But he was a guy, and guys didn't always share their feelings. Another little tidbit she knew. Not very useful, but something. "I can't imagine any woman who would walk away from you. She must've been insane."

His bark of laughter cut through the silence in the room. "That was the problem. She was insane."

Jane reached out a hand and took his in hers. "Then you're better off without her."

His fingers tightened around hers. "That is an understatement. I know I'm better off without her. My entire family is better off without her."

"You have siblings?" Jane asked, hoping to steer him away from a painful past with his ex-wife.

"I have a sister. You might know of her…." His gaze met hers. "Sadie McClain."

The way Fin looked at her expectantly, Jane felt like she should know the name. Though she racked her brain, she couldn't come up with a face to match the name. Finally, she shook her head. "Sorry. I don't know her."

He grinned. "That's a first."

Jane's eyebrows drew together. "What do you mean?"

"Nothing. Just that, I swear, everyone knows Sadie."

"I'm sorry. Maybe if I saw a picture of her…?" Jane offered.

Fin pulled his cellphone out of his back pocket and thumbed through his photos until he stopped on one. He held his phone out to her.

She studied the photo carefully.

Posing in front of a sprawling house was a beautiful blue-eyed blonde standing beside a man with dark hair and impossibly broad shoulders. She held a baby on her hip, and he balanced a little girl in the crook of his arm. They were all smiling.

Jane sighed at their happiness. "Your sister is beautiful. Her family is beautiful. You're fortunate." Something about them tugged at her heart.

Did she have siblings? Dear God. What kind of sister was she if she forgot her siblings? How did someone do that?

That feeling of overwhelming loss washed over her. It was as if losing her memory made her lose every person she'd ever loved. She had to have loved someone.

She held onto the cellphone, her grip tight, her eyes swimming. "My family has to be out there somewhere. It can't be just me. It doesn't feel right."

"Any faces come to mind?" Fin asked as he took the cellphone from her fingers.

Jane shook her head. "Nothing. My mind is like a deep dark room, and I'm standing in the doorway, staring into the shadows. If I could just take a step into that room, the light should come on, right?" She thought hard, willing herself to go through that door, to take that step. Her head hurt with the effort. Her frustration deepened when she couldn't get past that mental block holding her back from her past.

Still holding one of her hands with his, Fin reached out and cupped her cheek. "Don't try so hard. You might be sabotaging your recovery by placing more stress and strain on an injured brain." He bent and pressed a kiss to her forehead.

It was featherlight and felt nice, stirring in her a desire for more than just the brush of his lips on her forehead. The small gesture sent warmth to coil around her core, building like a slow-burning flame in a light summer breeze.

He stared down at her, his blue eyes very much like his sister's, pale and beautiful. This man who'd rescued her from where she'd lain in the middle of the highway had gone above and beyond, remaining with her when he probably had better places to be.

He held himself straight. His hair was short, and his bearing was that of someone who'd spent time in the military. He was strong, kind and gentle with a stranger he didn't have to stay with but did.

Jane felt an overwhelming sense of gratitude that he had been her island in a sea of uncertainty. But she felt so much more than gratitude. She felt a primitive longing that had nothing to do with gratitude. The man was ruggedly handsome with shadows in his blue eyes. She wanted to know what had caused those shadows. And she wanted to touch him, to feel the skin stretched tightly across his broad chest.

Jane reached up, cupped his cheeks in her palms, and kissed him full on the lips. "Thank you, soldier."

He stiffened against her.

She leaned back in time to see his eyes flash. Then it was as if they became hooded.

She opened her mouth to apologize for kissing him, but she closed it before uttering the words. She wasn't sorry. Jane liked the way his lips felt against hers. A kind of warm familiarity. Almost as if she'd felt them before.

She looked into his eyes.

He stared back as if willing her to notice something. What, she had no clue.

The doctor saved her from uttering something stupid like, *Do you know me, and you're not letting on?*

Indeed, if he did know her, he wouldn't have given the receptionist the name of Jane Doe.

"I'm Dr. Rhodes." The man in the white coat introduced himself and shined a penlight into her eyes, one at a time. "I understand you've been involved in an accident?"

She nodded and blinked at the light. "I guess."

"The nurse tells me you don't remember anything before the accident." He listened to her heart and lungs then pressed his fingers gently into her abdomen. "Does that hurt?"

"No."

"Where do you hurt?" he asked and stood back for her answer.

She pointed to the sore spot on her head and to a few places on her arms and legs where her fall had ripped holes in her jacket and pants.

The doctor had her remove the jacket with Fin's help. Beneath it, she wore a short-sleeved black T-shirt. Several bruises were starting to turn blue and purple on her arms.

After a thorough exam, the doctor ordered a CT scan.

Jane was wheeled to radiology. When she came back, the doctor already had the results from the radiologist. "No bleeding on the brain, and your skull remains intact, but your loss of memory, dizziness and headache indicates concussion. I want to keep you overnight for observation."

Jane shook her head. "I don't want to stay."

"You have a concussion," Fin said. "Some

people, who hit their heads and feel fine, end up dying a few hours later. I'd feel better if you stayed the night and let them watch you."

Jane bit down hard on her tongue to keep from asking Fin if he would stay with her. He didn't have to be with her now. Why would he stay with a perfect stranger overnight? No. She wouldn't ask. Her weakness throughout the time she'd known Fin wasn't like her. Deep inside, she knew she was stronger than how she'd been since waking up in the arms of this man as he'd lifted her off the pavement.

The void of her memories made her cling to him, and she couldn't do that. He had a home he needed to get to. Arguing with the doctor would make Fin feel like he had to stay.

"Okay. I'll stay the night," she said to the doctor.

He nodded. "I'll let the nurse know to secure a room." He left the room.

When the door closed behind the doctor, Jane turned to Fin. "I'll stay the night, only if you promise to go home. I can't keep making you stay. You have your own life. I'll be fine. I don't need a babysitter. I've already delayed you enough."

His lips quirked on the corners. "I wouldn't have stayed if I didn't want to."

Jane couldn't imagine Fin doing anything he

didn't want to, which made her feel marginally better. "Still, you were on the way to somewhere when you came across me. I can't keep you from getting to where you were going." She smiled. "Where were you going?"

His hint of a smile slipped. "To see my sister, Sadie."

Guilt pinched hard in her chest. "I'm sorry. She must be beside herself worried about you."

"She's not. I told her I'd get to her place either late tonight or early tomorrow. So, she won't be worried until I don't show up tomorrow. And I can allay her concerns with a phone call if I'm any later."

Jane's eyes narrowed. "Seriously, I won't stay if you don't go."

He grinned. "Are you trying to get rid of me?"

Hell, no. She wanted him to stay more than she wanted to take her next breath. "I want you to go. You've wasted enough time with me. At least, go to your sister's place for a good night's sleep. I'll be asleep most of the night. It's not like I'll need you here." She held up her hands. "Not that I haven't appreciated everything you've done for me. I'll feel guilty if you don't see your sister, and you tell her I'm sorry for delaying you."

Still, he hesitated.

Jane sighed. "Just go. I need to let my body rest."

His lips pressed together in a thin line. "When a person saves the life of another person, he's responsible for that person's life. I don't feel right leaving you."

"I don't feel right having you stay." She crossed her arms over her chest. "I do want you to go to your sister's place and apologize to her and her family."

Fin winced at her words.

"It shouldn't hurt that bad," Jane said. "I am sorry for holding you up from visiting your family."

He nodded. "I'll go as soon as I see you settled in a room."

Her lips twisted. "Don't trust that I'll stay?"

He nodded. "You didn't want to come to the hospital in the first place."

She held up her hand. "I promise that I'll stay."

"Okay. But I'm still staying until you're moved to your room. I want to know where to find you when I come back."

Her heart swelled with hope. He was coming back. "In that case, I'll be here when you do."

An orderly arrived to wheel her to her room.

Fin walked alongside her all the way and

waited outside the door as a nurse helped her change into a nightgown and settle in the sheets.

When the nurse left, Fin entered. "Good," he said. "You won't be running off in a hospital gown."

"I told you I'd stay." *Especially if you're coming back.* She didn't add that out loud, afraid it would make her sound too desperate. Which she was. The thought of Fin walking out the door petrified her. If he didn't come back, what would happen to her? She had no place to go.

"Okay." Fin glanced around the room once more. "Are you sure you'll be all right?"

No.

She nodded.

He grabbed a pad and pen from the nightstand beside her bed and jotted down a phone number. "Call me if you need me. Hell, call me even if you don't. I'll answer as long as I have cellphone reception. It's hit and miss outside of town. If I don't answer, leave a message. I'll call back." He reached for her hand. "You're not alone. I will be back in the morning."

Her eyes burned with a wash of tears she refused to release. Her throat thickened until all she could do was nod.

Fin squeezed her fingers and bent to brush his lips across hers.

Then he was gone.

The emptiness of the room threatened to pull Jane into the deepest darkest place she'd ever known.

The one shining light was the promise of Fin returning the following day.

She clung to the promise like a drowning victim clinging to a life-saving buoy.

CHAPTER 3

As FIN RODE the elevator to the ground floor, he almost pushed the button to stop and get out. He didn't want to leave her. Her sense of guilt for having taken up so much of his time was groundless. He had wanted to help her, wanted to stay and make sure she was okay.

He couldn't imagine what it was like to lose your memory. But just seeing the confusion, fear and misery in her eyes gave him enough of a clue to know she was not in a good place. She had nothing and no one without knowing who she was and where she belonged.

He'd give her the night to recuperate, then he'd be back, hopefully with a plan as to what to do next.

His sister's husband was a former Navy SEAL

with his own protection service and computer guy. Maybe they could help figure out who Jane was and get her back to her home.

In the meantime, if she truly was in danger, they might be able to offer her the protection she needed.

As he stepped out into the lobby of the Emergency Room, he noticed a commotion at the sliding glass doors.

A couple of guys carried a man between them who was bruised and bloody.

"We need help here," one called out, pausing in the open doorway, blocking the exit.

The receptionist ducked into the restricted area and emerged a couple of seconds later, pushing a wheelchair. "What happened?"

"There was an accident on the interstate just before the exit," one man said as he helped the other ease the guy in the middle down into the wheelchair.

The injured man winced.

"We called 9-1-1, but we were close enough to get this guy here. I think the ambulance is on its way for those who are more seriously injured. They're going to have to pry some of the victims out of their vehicles." He shook his head. "It's bad."

A man in a hoodie slid in behind them through

the sliding glass doors, carrying a camera. He stood in front of the man in the wheelchair and snapped several photos. "Are you one of the victims of the pileup?"

The man groaned, his head lolling.

As she attempted to push the wheelchair toward the door leading back to the exam rooms, the nurse frowned at the guy with the camera. "Go home, Will. Can't you see the guy is in pain?"

"Yeah, but I could use some comments from one or two of those injured to go along with my story."

"You still posting trash on your social media?" the nurse asked as she tried again to get around him.

"No way. I'm selling stories to the local news channel."

Her frown deepened. "Go home, Will."

Will stood straighter, his chin tipping up. "I got just as much right to be in this hospital as anyone."

"That's right," the nurse finally pushed past him. "As long as you don't disturb the patients."

"I'm not disturbing the patients," Will said. "I'm here for the story."

"Then go up to the crash site." The nurse entered the doors marked restricted and let the doors swing shut between her and Will.

Will turned to the receptionist. "Hey, Michelle, any interesting cases come your way tonight?"

Michelle frowned. "You know I can't discuss patients. It's against HIPAA standards."

Will leaned over the desk and smiled. "Oh, come on. You can tell me."

Fin fought the urge to roll his eyes. The reporter didn't give up, did he?

Fin didn't have time to stand around. He wanted to get to the White Oak Ranch before it got much later. As it was, they might already be in bed. He contemplated staying in Bozeman as was his original plan until he'd met Jane. Now, he didn't want to stay in a hotel. He wanted to camp out in Jane's room to keep an eye on her. Since he couldn't do that, he needed to get to Sadie's place and enlist the help of Hank's organization, the Brotherhood Protectors, to help him discover who Jane Doe was. He wished he'd snapped a photo of her to take with him. Maybe Hank's computer guy had a way of tapping into facial recognition databases.

As he left the hospital, and before he left Bozeman, he placed a call to Sadie.

"Hey, Fin, when are you getting here?"

"I'll be there in an hour," he said. "Do you need anything from Bozeman before I leave town?"

"No, we're well-stocked."

"Is Hank home? Or is he off providing protection or security to some wealthy celebrity?"

Sadie laughed. "He has a full staff now and pretty much runs the show and lets them take on the assignments. He does fill in when it takes a team effort. So, yeah, he's home. Do you want to talk to him?"

"Yes, when I get there. I have a potential client for him."

"Really?" A baby cooed in the background. "Hey, Mac, you're finally going to meet your Uncle Fin." Then without missing a beat, she asked, "Who is she?"

He laughed. "How do you know it's a *she*?"

"Lucky guess," Sadie said. "Do I know her?"

"No," he said. "I'll fill you and Hank in when I get there. I'm driving out of Bozeman, and I don't know how long I'll have reception."

"Okay. I'll let Hank know to stay up late. You do realize it'll be close to midnight by the time you get here…?"

"Sorry about that. I was waylaid on my drive into Bozeman."

"Which I'm sure is a story in itself. See you soon, brother. And it's about time you came home."

He ended the call, glad to hear his sister's voice

and dreading seeing her a little less. He had a purpose for visiting home. Not that it was anything like the home he'd known growing up. The original ranch house had burned to the ground. The fire had almost taken Sadie with it.

He wasn't sorry the old house was gone. It held too many memories of his life with Carla and what she'd tried to do to Sadie.

Sadie and Hank had built a new, beautiful house with a basement bunker where Hank had set up shop for the Brotherhood Protectors. In it, he'd collected all the latest computer and communications equipment and an armory that would make any active-duty special operations soldier or SEAL envious.

Fin hadn't seen it, having been gone now for five years. Sadie had sent pictures and kept him up to date on the changes, along with pictures of his niece and nephew.

Guilt tugged at his gut. He didn't know Sadie's children. And they didn't know him. Would they be afraid of him? Hell, he shouldn't have stayed away so long.

He hadn't had a choice. His head hadn't been in the right place for most of that five years. He'd been hellbent on taking point and charging into every battle first. Maybe his zeal had been a kind of suicide attempt or an adrenaline rush. Or perhaps he was trying to make up for being blind to his ex-wife's murderous ways. More than likely, it had been a way to punish himself.

Whatever, he'd been reckless with his own life, while trying not to put the lives of his teammates in unnecessary danger. He'd volunteered for all the high-risk missions and by some twist of fate, had lived through all of them.

It hadn't been his time to go.

After nearly running over Jane Doe, he could begin to believe he hadn't died because he still had a purpose in this life. That purpose might be to help Jane. Hell, she didn't have anyone else.

An hour after he'd left Jane at the hospital, he pulled up to the gate of the ranch and punched in the code on the keypad.

The gate slid open, and he drove his truck through it, following the winding path through the trees and up a hill. When he emerged from the dark forest, he grinned at the sight of the beautiful home Sadie and Hank had built for themselves. Every light appeared to be shining brightly from the windows and on the porch.

Hank and Sadie stepped out of the house onto the deck, smiling.

Even with shadows cast on their faces, they

appeared happy. Sadie's cheeks glowed with health, and her grin spread practically from ear to ear.

Yeah, he shouldn't have stayed gone so long.

He and Sadie were only two years apart in age. Their relationship growing up had been tighter than most teens, and they'd leaned on each other through the deaths of their parents.

He'd been so proud of her when she'd set off to make a name for herself in Hollywood, cheering her on after every audition and callback.

When she'd made it big, he couldn't have been prouder of his little sister.

And now, she stood in the circle of Hank's arm, leaning into him, happier than Fin had ever seen her.

He climbed the steps, barely reaching the top before Sadie flung her arms around his shoulders and hugged him so tightly, he couldn't breathe. And he didn't care. He could die right there and know he'd been happy reuniting with his sister.

When she finally leaned back, there were tears in her eyes. "Welcome home, Fin."

He looked around at the beautiful rock and cedar house with the massive windows overlooking the Crazy Mountains. It wasn't home to him. Not the house.

But the shadowy mountains in the distance... They were a permanent part of his being. Every time he looked at them, he stood in awe of their beauty and majesty. He had missed them.

"Come inside," Hank said. "Sadie's made a pot of hot cocoa."

"Unless you want something stronger." Sadie glanced up at him, raising her eyebrows.

He smiled. "Cocoa sounds great. As long as you have marshmallows."

Sadie laughed. "Cocoa isn't cocoa without marshmallows. At least, according to Emma."

Fin followed them through the door into the vast expanse of the living room with its twenty-foot ceiling overhead and a massive stone fireplace with a wood fire burning brightly in it.

"Where are Emma and McClain?" he asked, looking around the room.

Sadie shook her head. "They go down around eight o'clock and are up bright and early between five-thirty and six."

Hank chuckled. "Don't worry. You'll get to hear them as well as see them."

"I look forward to getting to know them."

They walked together into the kitchen a professional chef would have been proud to cook in. Sadie crossed to the pot on the gas stove and fired up the flame beneath it. "It's warm, so it won't take long to get hot. You two can get the cheese out of the fridge and cut some slices."

A small television hung from beneath an upper cabinet, the late-night news flashing images and video clips, the sound on mute.

Hank opened the refrigerator and pulled out three different blocks of cheese. He set it on a cutting board and cut off several slices, laying them on a platter. He nodded to a door behind Fin. "There are boxes of crackers in the pantry. Pick what you like."

Fin didn't care about what kind of crackers to pick. He grabbed the closest box and placed it on the counter beside Hank.

"Sadie says you have a potential client for me," Hank said.

"Maybe. I don't know how your operation works. I only know this woman might need protection.

"Who is she?" Hank asked.

Sadie snorted softly and murmured in Hank's ear. "Good luck on that one."

Fin shook his head. "It's not that I don't want to tell you. I just don't know. Nor does she."

Hank and Sadie's brows descended.

"What do you mean?" Hank asked.

"She doesn't remember who she is, where she's from or what brought her to Montana."

Hank stared hard into Fin's eyes. "Are you sure she's not faking it?"

Fin shook his head and tore open a package of crackers, laying a handful on the platter. "She's not. I found her on Interstate 90 an hour northwest of Bozeman. She stumbled out into the road and passed out. I think she'd been in an accident."

"Did you get a look at her vehicle?"

"No," Fin's lips twisted. "She'd hit her head and had blood running down the side of her face as well as other scratches and bruises. I was more worried about getting her to a hospital than taking the time to look for her vehicle."

Hank's brow puckered. "And she doesn't remember anything?"

Fin took the knife from Hank's hands and finished slicing the cheese. "Nothing before waking up on the highway." He carried the platter to the table.

Sadie joined him with a tray of mugs filled with steaming hot cocoa and a bowl of puffy miniature marshmallows. "Do you think someone threw her out onto the highway?"

"I don't know." Fin selected one of the mugs and poured a healthy helping of marshmallows from the bowl onto the creamy cocoa. "And that seems to be the recurring theme for the evening."

"If you can give me an approximate location of where you were when you found her, I'll send someone out to search for her vehicle."

"It would be like searching for a needle in a haystack. We were in the Beaverhead-Deerlodge National Forest. I was about to round a large curve in the interstate when I saw her, and we were still an hour out of Bozeman. Other than that, I couldn't tell you an exact coordinate."

Hank nodded. "Gotcha. I know someone who might be able to help. One of the guys who works for the brotherhood, Kujo, is married to a woman who works for the regional office of the FBI here in Montana. She's getting good at flying her drone. She might be able to spot the vehicle from the air. And Kujo has a retired Military Working Dog, Six. He might be able to track her path from where she ended up on the road to where her car landed. Let me handle that."

"It would help if we could get a license plate or registration papers from her vehicle," Fin said. "She'd feel a lot better knowing her name at the very least."

"Did she not have any identification on her?" Sadie asked.

Fin shook his head. "Nothing. Not even a receipt in her pocket. They checked her into the hospital as Jane Doe." He'd hated that, but what choice had he had? "It was better than calling her *that woman* or *hey you.*"

Sadie lifted her mug and blew on the hot liquid before taking a tentative sip. "I can only imagine how frustrating and frightening it must be to lose one's memories. I would be devastated if I couldn't remember that I had Hank, Emma and McClain."

Fin stared across at her. "You wouldn't know you even had them. They'd be even more frantic trying to find you. I wonder if Jane's family is looking for her."

"I can have my guy Swede tap into the police database for missing persons."

"It might be too soon for her family to file a missing person report," Fin pointed out.

"True, but I'll have him look anyway and look again every five hours or more."

"Thanks," Fin said and downed his drink, scalding his throat. "I feel like I should've stayed at the hospital. Jane insisted I go home. She was going to sleep."

"Are you worried she'll walk away?" Hank asked.

"I'm not sure. Where would she go? She doesn't

know anyone or if she has a home in the Bozeman area."

"Would it help if they posted a photo of her on the local news to see if someone recognizes her?" Sadie asked.

"That's just it." Fin stood and walked to the sink with his empty glass. "When I told her I was taking her to the hospital, she immediately said no. She was still dazed and confused, so I didn't think anything of it. When I asked her why she said, *they'll find me.*" He turned. "Could someone have followed her and run her off the road?"

"Or could someone have dumped her?" Sadie repeated her hypothesis.

"Like you said...." Hank stared across the table at Fin, "she might need protection."

"Do you have anyone available?" Fin asked.

"Not at this moment, but I could free up someone if you can give me a day or two. How long will she be in the hospital?"

"They'll release her in the morning. They're just keeping her for observation for a possible concussion."

"When she's released, bring her out here. I'll think of something." Hank finished his cocoa and strode toward the sink. "Can you turn up the volume on the television? The late weather report should be coming on soon."

Fin adjusted the volume as the news anchor segued into the next report, turning in her chair to face a different camera. "In local news, a mystery woman arrived at the hospital in Bozeman this evening, claiming she didn't know her name or where she was from. If anyone recognizes her, please contact the police or the hospital. Her family might be worried about her."

Fin stiffened at the woman's words. He cursed when a photo flashed on the screen of Jane lying in a hospital bed, her eyes closed, her dark hair splayed out on the bright white sheets.

"Holy hell." Hank pointed at the screen. "Is that her?"

Fin set his mug in the sink, so angry his hands shook. "Yes. What I'd like to know is the name of the bastard who took that photo while she was asleep in her room?" There had been a reporter in the lobby of the hospital as Fin had left. God, he wished he'd stayed. He turned to Sadie. "I have to go."

"You just got here." Sadie pouted. "But I get it. If someone did run her off the road, they might come back to finish the job." She waved a hand toward the door. "Go."

Hank pulled his cellphone out of his pocket and snapped a picture of the woman on the television screen right before the anchor reappeared. "If this image is clear enough, we can run it through whatever facial recognition software databases Swede can access. Maybe we'll get a hit."

"Thanks," Fin said. To Sadie, he added, "I'll be back. I'm on mandatory leave for two weeks. My commander said he'd court-martial me if I returned any sooner."

Sadie winced. "Did that have to do with the note I sent to the Red Cross?"

Fin nodded. "Yes, ma'am." Then he bent and kissed her cheek. "But I'm glad you did it. It was time I came home to my family."

"You know we love you," Sadie said. "White Oak Ranch is as much yours as mine. And it really would be a shame if Emma and Mac didn't get to know their terrific Uncle Fin." She gave him a gentle smile. "What happened in the past is just that...in the past. And it wasn't your fault. You have to believe that." She cupped his cheek in her hand. "I love you, brother. I want you to be a part of our lives."

His heart pinched hard in his chest. "I love you, too. I just didn't know how to make things right, so I avoided coming home."

"Things were made right when Carla went to jail," Hank said. "As long as she stays there, we're all good." He held out his hand. "You're family. You belong with us."

Fin took the man's hand and shook it. "Thank you." He still felt like a fool for missing all the signs of a criminally insane woman, but it helped to know Sadie and Hank wanted him there. He hadn't felt at home since he'd joined the Army shortly after Carla's conviction.

Coming back to the Crazy Mountains was as close to feeling like he'd come home as he was likely to get. And it felt good.

But a woman was lying in a hospital bed with a dumbass photojournalist sneaking snapshots of her.

"I shouldn't have left," he murmured as he hurried out the door, climbed into his truck and headed back down the highway he'd just traveled to get to Bozeman.

His foot pressed hard on the accelerator as he pushed his truck faster. What if Jane's premonition of someone finding her wasn't just the rambles of a brain-scrambled woman?

Hang in there, Angel...I'm coming.

CHAPTER 4

JANE DRIFTED in and out of sleep, her head throbbing and her stomach churning. She might have forgotten just about everything, but her gut told her she needed to get moving. She was supposed to do something important.

Every time she strained to remember even the smallest details, her head hurt worse.

During one microburst of sleep, she thought she heard the door open and close, but she was too out of it to open her eyes, even when she heard a muted click.

After spinning in and out of sleep for nearly two hours, she gave up and lay staring at the ceiling, willing the time to pass quickly so that morning would arrive, and she would see Fin again.

A nurse came in, checked her vitals and handed her a tiny cup with a pill. "Need a sleep aid?" she asked with a friendly smile. "Most patients find it hard to sleep in the hospital. The doctor prescribed this for you. It'll help you get a good night's sleep."

"I don't want it," Jane responded automatically.

The nurse glanced up at the clock on the wall. "You might reconsider. It's already midnight, and you're not asleep. If you want to get out of here in the morning, you need rest." She held out the tiny plastic cup and a larger one filled with ice water and a straw.

Rather than waste time arguing, Jane took the cup from the woman's hand, tossed the medicine into her mouth and chased it with a sip from the straw. Then she smiled. "Thank you." The pill lay beneath her tongue until the nurse left the room.

When the door closed and Jane was alone again, she spit the pill into a tissue and tossed it into the trash can beside the bed.

She didn't want any mediation that had the potential to dull her already scrambled senses.

Perhaps a small amount of sleep medication had leached into her tongue, or her mind and body had finally reached their limit. Whatever it was,

Jane finally closed her eyes and she drifted into a deeper sleep where dreams came and went.

She wasn't sure how long she'd been asleep when a soft sound nudged her awake enough to open her eyes.

Before she could comprehend what was happening, a pillow slammed down on her face and was held tightly over her. Whoever was holding the pillow over her face laid down on her body, trapping her arms against her sides.

Jane flailed and kicked, by couldn't get any leverage to pry herself free of her captor, and her air was quickly running out.

When she tried to breathe, all she did was suck the sheet fabric of the pillowcase into her nose and mouth.

She tried to scream, but the sound was completely muffled by the pillow.

Though she fought hard, she couldn't break free. The man on top of her was heavier and had all the control with her pinned beneath him.

Without oxygen, her struggles became weaker and her thoughts muzzy. Was this it? Would she die in a hospital bed, murdered under the noses of the nurses and doctors there to help her?

She succumbed to the darkness, giving in to the superior strength of the man holding her down.

Her last thought as she passed out was the highly disappointing realization that she wouldn't get to see Fin McClain again.

FIN ARRIVED at the hospital in less than an hour, having sped like a maniac on the crooked highway between White Oak Ranch and the Bozeman hospital.

No state police, sheriff's deputies or any other law enforcement vehicle blasted out of the woodwork to slow him down, for which Fin was eternally grateful.

When the elevator proved too slow for his liking, Fin took the stairs two at a time until he reached Jane's floor. He burst through the stairwell door onto the clean, polished tiles, slowed his pace only slightly, and then ran to Jane's assigned room.

Pushing quietly through the door, he peeked around the edge of the door for a glimpse of Jane.

Instead, he saw a man dressed all in black with a black mask over his face, leaning all his weight over the bed, smashing a pillow between him and whatever was lying beneath him.

Adrenaline spiked through Fin's veins. "Hey! What the hell?"

The man's head shot up, but he didn't let go of the pillow.

Fin hunched low and charged at the man. He slammed into him like he'd hit dozens of quarterbacks when he'd played football a hundred years ago in high school.

The man crashed into the wall and slid to the floor. Fin gripped his jacket collar, lifted him off the floor and punched him full in the face. Again, the man hit the floor, only this time, he lay still.

Fin turned to the bed and yanked the pillow off Jane's face. She lay still, pale and unresponsive. His heart pounding in his chest, Fin hit the call button on the side of the bed, fear ripping through him. What if he hadn't been in time to save her?

Fear exploded into anger. His gaze shifted from Jane to the man lying on the floor. But anger wouldn't get Jane breathing again.

He covered her mouth with his and blew air into her lungs watching as her chest rose and fell.

"That's right," he said. "Out with the old. In with the new." He blew into her mouth again and felt for a pulse. After a long moment, he felt it.

While he worked over Jane, coaxing her to breathe on her own, he wondered where the hell the nurses were.

Focused on Jane, he didn't see her assailant

crawl toward the door until he scrambled to his feet and pushed through the swinging door out into the hallway where two nurses were on their way in.

He shoved through them, knocking one of them down in his hurry to get away.

"Call security," Fin yelled. "We need to stop that man. He tried to kill Jane."

The nurse still on her feet raced to the nurses' station and made the call. The one on the floor got to her feet and hurried into the room with Fin.

"She has a pulse. It's faint, but steady," Fin said.

The nurse grabbed a ventilation bag, covered Jane's nose and mouth and gently squeezed the bag, forcing air in and out of Jane's lungs.

After a couple of minutes, Jane gasped. Her hands shot up and shoved the bag and the nurse away. She sat up straight on the bed and dragged in deep gulps of air, her eyes wide and frightened.

When her troubled gaze landed on Fin, she cried out. "Fin!"

He went to her, wrapped his arms around her and held her as her body trembled. He wished he'd killed the man who'd done this to her instead of leaving him to live another day. He was a cold-hearted bastard who didn't deserve to breathe the same air as his Angel.

"I...c-couldn't...breathe," Jane whispered.

His heart contracted. Amnesia and almost being smothered...Jane had been through hell.

Smoothing a hand over her dark hair, he spoke softly. "You can breathe now. Take slow, deep breaths. Do it with me." He leaned back enough to look down into her face. Then he sucked in a lungful of air.

She followed suit.

When he let it out slowly, she did as well.

They repeated the process several times before he asked, "Better?"

"Yes." Still, she didn't let go of his hand. Her gaze met his. "You came back."

He nodded. "Did you authorize someone to take a picture of you and put it up on the local news channel?"

She shook her head. "No. Of course not."

"Well, someone did, and he aired it on the local news station asking if anyone knew who you were."

Her hand clenched around his. "Damn."

"You were right. Someone found you. Hopefully, security caught him before he left the building."

"I'll check," the nurse said as she gathered the ventilation bag and left the room.

"I'm sorry I've taken up so much of your time," Jane stared down at where their hands were joined. Then she looked up into his eyes. "But thank you for saving me again."

He leaned forward and pressed his lips to her forehead. "I'm just glad I got here in time."

"Me, too." Jane touched a hand to his chest. "Will you be going back to your family tonight?"

"Hell, no," he responded. "I'm staying here with you. I never should've left."

"I'm not your responsibility," she said. "Normally, I can take care of myself." Her brow dipped low. "Why do I know that?" She shook her head and sighed. "I haven't been a good example of self-reliance since you met me."

"You have good reason for the lapse. Whatever accident you had was significant. You have to give yourself time to heal."

"I might not have time," she whispered.

"I won't let anything happen to you. I'm staying right here."

She lay back on the bed, her eyes drifting closed. "How will you sleep?"

He chuckled. "With one eye open."

She scooted over on the bed and patted the space beside her. "There's enough room for both of us."

"As good as that sounds, I'll pull up a chair. You need to rest. You've been through a lot. Sleep."

She snorted. "I'm so tired, but when I close my eyes, I feel like that pillow is smothering me all over again. Can a person sleep with her eyes open?"

"Guess you won't know until you try." He smiled. "I once fell asleep standing up."

Jane could picture the big guy leaning against a wall, asleep, and she smiled. "That takes talent."

"We do what you have to," Fin said. "When we're in a war zone, sleep is a luxury."

"Yes, it is." As soon as the words left her mouth, she paused.

"You say that like you've lived it," Fin said.

"Yet, I can't remember ever being in a war." She stared down at her hospital gown. "And I sure as hell haven't acted like it." Meeting his gaze, she tilted her head. "Was I in the military?" She shook her head. "I don't feel like I ever wore a uniform." Jane sighed, laid back against the pillow and stared up at the ceiling without blinking for a few minutes. Eventually, she closed her eyes.

The scrape of metal across the floor made her glance his way.

He'd scooted a chair close to the bed.

She liked that. It made her feel safer having him

so close. All she had to do was reach out and she'd touch him.

He took her hand in his and laced their fingers together. "What's your favorite color?" he asked.

"Blue," she answered without hesitation, the laughed. "Why can I remember something so inconsequential as a favorite color, but I can't remember my name?"

"Favorite flower?" He quizzed.

"Bluebonnets in Texas," she answered and smiled. "Again, unimportant."

"Why bluebonnets?" Fin asked.

"I love the way they can fill an entire field. The purply blue is so bright and beautiful with the promise of spring. Add splashes of orange Indian paintbrush flowers scattered in the sea of bluish-purple and you have a perfect setting for a picnic."

"Maybe we're getting somewhere." Fin leaned forward, their hands still entwined. "We can assume you've been to Texas in the springtime."

Jane nodded. "If flashes of fields of bluebonnets are an indication, then yes. But there wasn't much else."

"But you're remembering," Fin insisted. "You like the color blue and bluebonnets. It's a start."

"With a very long way to go."

"Maybe once you start remembering on a larger scale, it will all rush back in."

"I can only hope." Jane closed her eyes again. "Did you see your sister?" she asked.

"I did."

"I bet she wasn't happy when you left almost as soon as you got there."

"She was very understanding when I explained the situation. I told her I'd be back."

She touched his hand. "I'm sorry."

"Don't be." He slid his hand across her arm. "I'm almost positive you didn't ask to be wandering around on the highway in the middle of nowhere."

"You didn't ask to be the first on the scene," she countered.

"You have to bet that fate played a hand in bringing us together at that exact moment for a reason. It wasn't your time to die."

"And it was *your* time to be saddled with a woman who can't remember her name?" Jane shook her head. "Fate can be tricky. For all you know, I could be a mass murderer."

He smiled. "For all you know, I could be the same."

Jane chuckled. "We'd make a great pair in that case."

"So, I'd commit the crimes?" He shook his head.

A grin spread across her face. "I'd drive the getaway vehicle." Her grin faded. "You don't strike me as someone who'd commit mass murder."

"However, you do strike me as someone who could drive the getaway car." Fin stared at her for a long moment. "Or motorcycle," he added.

Something tickled at the back of my mind. She wasn't sure what it was.

"Have I ridden a motorcycle?" she wondered aloud. "Was that why I was dressed in a leather jacket and pants?"

Fin's eyes narrowed, and he took a long time to reply, finally saying, "Makes sense. Then again, you don't have any skulls or words on your leather, so I can assume you aren't a member of a motorcycle club. Or you're so new, you haven't earned your letters."

"Not my style," she said automatically. "I know that. I just don't dig deep to get these little sound bites of my memory," she said. "They just come to me." She pinched the bridge of her nose as if that would help her concentrate and force out the memories that remained elusive.

"Don't stress over it," Fin said. "Your memories will come back when they're good and ready."

"Since I don't have any memories, could you share a few of yours?" She smiled. "Please."

"What do you want to know? My first visit from the tooth fairy? What my mother dressed me as for Halloween when I was four? You already know my favorite sports team."

"How about your favorite memory of your parents?" she asked.

He tilted his head. "That would have to be the time we went as a family to the state park in Arkansas to dig for diamonds." He stared across at her. "Did you know there is an open field where you could find and keep diamonds here in the US?"

She shook her head. "I doubt, even if I had my memories back, that I would've known that." Jane studied Fin. "Did you find a diamond?"

He laughed. "No. But it had just rained. The field was one giant mud pit. After only an hour, we were covered from head to toe in mud. Even my mother, the woman who didn't like to get dirt under her fingernails, was up to her earlobes in thick Arkansas mud. I'd never seen her smile so much and sling mud at us kids after we'd fallen for the hundredth time."

His smile continued long after his story ended. "I never knew playing in the mud could bring a family even closer together."

Jane drew in a deep breath and let it out. It

didn't help to ease the pain of the void in her life. Maybe it was a blessing that she didn't know what she'd lost. Good or bad. In the meantime, she had new memories to make and possibly enjoy. The present and the future were still hers and she didn't have a problem remembering since her accident.

Her gaze sought Fin's. When and if her memories returned, and she went back to where she belonged, would she ever see Fin again?

He'd been amazingly kind and gentle with her, taking care of her when she was down. Would he be as attentive when she was on her own two feet? She knew, deep down, she was a strong woman. Her injuries were the only thing holding her back.

Would Fin feel threatened by a woman who could take care of herself?

Jane felt like she'd run into men who were threatened by women who were smarter, stronger and better marksmen than they were. Was that who she was? Smarter, stronger and a better marksman than most men?

She thought hard about it.

Maybe.

Why would she think she was a better marksman than most men? Had she been put to the test? Had she been in the military?

The more questions she asked herself, the more frustrated she became.

At the back of her mind, a nagging feeling tugged at her gut. She needed to be somewhere soon.

Damn it!

Where?

CHAPTER 5

AFTER THE BOZEMAN police department had come and questioned them about the man who thought killing Jane was a good idea, Jane fell asleep pretty quickly.

Fin stayed awake well into the early hours of the morning, finally falling asleep with his head resting on the bed beside his and Jane's joined hands.

He didn't wake until a nurse came in to take Jane's vitals, waking her as well.

Jane's eyes blinked open, and she yawned, stretching beneath the sheet and hospital blanket. "When am I getting out of here?" she asked the nurse.

The nurse grinned. "What? Don't you like the accommodations?" She winked.

"The staff here has been exceptional. I appreciate everything you all have done for me," Jane said.

"I hear a *but* coming," the nurse said as she fill out Jane's electronic chart.

"But...I'm not sick, and I'm barely injured." She shrugged. "A few bruises never killed someone. I can live with them. I need to get out of this place. The sooner, the better."

Fin's lips quirked upward. "Have you thought about where you'll go?"

Jane nodded slowly in the affirmative and then shook her head. "No."

"I have a suggestion."

"Since I don't," she said, "I'm listening."

"I want you to meet my sister and her husband."

Jane frowned. "Why would you do that? I'm a stranger. You don't know anything about me. Hell. I don't know anything about me. I could be a threat to your family."

"I think you are more threatened than a threat." Fin took her hand in his and stared into her eyes. "Last night was proof of that. I can't, in good conscience, walk away from you. Once you save a life—"

"—you're responsible for that life." Jane shook

her head. "I'm telling you…you're not responsible for me. I can take care of myself."

He cocked an eyebrow. "Do you have any money?"

Her lips pressed into a thin line. "I'll get a job."

"What are you qualified to do?" he persisted.

"Something. Anything. I can cook or clean if nothing else. The point is, you're not responsible for me."

"And if that guy who tried to kill you last night finds you and tries to finish the job, who is going to help you."

"I'll be fine," she said. "I'll figure it out. Maybe there's a shelter somewhere nearby. I can stay there until my memory returns."

"No," Fin said.

This time Jane's eyebrows rose. "No?"

"No," Fin repeated. "You're not going to a homeless shelter. You can stay with me until I go back to Fort Lewis. Then I'm sure Hank will have somewhere you can stay until your memory returns."

The nurse finished tapping her fingers on the keyboard and faced Jane. "Do you need anything?"

"Breakfast?" Jane said, her stomach telling her and anyone else in earshot just how hungry she was.

The nurse grinned. "The trays will be here shortly."

"Good. That will give me time to dress and be ready for when the doc arrives." Jane threw back the blanket and sheet.

"You might want to wait until he releases you before you change into your street clothes," the nurse called out from the door.

"I'm leaving today," Jane said with certainty.

The moment the nurse left, another member of the staff entered carrying a tray of food, including a steaming cup of coffee.

Jane sat forward in the bed and pulled the table and tray over to where she could reach its contents.

Fin's mouth watered. He'd have to go down to the hospital cafeteria to get a cup of coffee.

Jane's glance skimmed over the contents of the tray. "I'm not much of a coffee drinker. Do you want it?"

"I thought you'd never ask." He scooped the pathetically small cup of coffee off the tray and sipped its contents, letting the adequate flavor slide down his throat and wake him the rest of the way to start the day.

Between the two of them, they cleaned the breakfast tray, each liking something different.

When it came to the eggs, Jane divided them down the middle.

"You really should be eating all of this," Fin said as he polished off a piece of toast. "You're the patient, not me."

She smiled. "It was more food than a normal human can consume. I'm glad you got something to eat." Pushing back the empty tray, she slipped out of the bed and stood barefoot on the floor, searching the room with her gaze.

"What are you looking for?" Fin asked.

"My clothes?"

"In the closet in the corner," he directed.

"Thank you." Jane found the closet, opened the door and pulled out the torn leather pants, T-shirt, panties and her bra. She entered the private bathroom off her room and closed the door.

Within five minutes, she'd showered, dressed in her dirty clothes and emerged. "I feel only marginally better," she said, staring down at the rips in the clothes. "But it's better than leaving the hospital in one of their gowns."

"We'll see what we can do to get you some clothes," Fin said.

Jane paced the room five times.

Still no doctor.

"How long will we have to wait?" she asked of the nurse who entered through the swinging door.

"About two seconds." The nurse turned toward the man entering the room behind her.

After a cursory exam, the doctor pronounced she could go home.

Fin winced. Where was home for the stranger he'd found on the interstate highway?

The nurse gave Jane an instruction sheet with signs and symptoms to look for with a head injury.

Practically chomping at the bit, Jane was the first person out the door.

Fin had to run to keep up with her. He reached out and caught her arm, holding it gently.

"I don't like hospitals," Jane said. "They give me the heebie-jeebies. It seems only bad things happen in hospitals."

Fin tucked that nugget of her returned memories into the back of his mind. Bit by bit, she was remembering. Before long, all of her memories would return. Until then, Fin would be by her side.

"So, are you coming with me?" he asked as they stepped out of the hospital into the cool morning air.

She stood for a moment, her face lifted to the sunshine. For a long moment, she didn't answer.

Then she faced him with a grimace. "I don't have much choice, do I?"

He snorted. "You don't have to come."

She gave him a weak smile. "Don't get me wrong. I appreciate all you've done for me. I just want to solve the mystery of who I am and why I'm in Montana. I don't think I live here." Her gaze went to the nearby mountains. "Although it's beautiful and has great potential as a place to live, I don't think I live here."

"Maybe not, but for the time being, you'll have to make do with fresh mountain air and sunshine."

She smiled. "Sounds like a hardship."

He cupped her elbow and guided her to the parking lot. "If you'll come with me, we'll get going. It takes an hour to get from here to my sister's place near Eagle Rock in the Crazy Mountains."

"Crazy Mountains?" her brow wrinkled. "Is this a place I should be going, given my insane condition?" She laughed. "Then again, I might as well. I'll fit right in." Jane fell in step beside him.

Fin was glad she could see the humor in her situation and that she wasn't crying about her memory loss. She accepted it as a matter of fact for the present while searching for ways to jog those memories loose. Some people, men or women, would fall completely apart if they lost what she'd lost.

He found himself liking Jane Doe more and more. That could be dangerous, considering he was not a good judge of character. The last relationship he'd been in had nearly cost his sister's life.

Was he inviting trouble by bringing this stranger into his family's home? He prayed she wasn't a mass murderer and that she really was good like his instinct was telling him.

When they reached his truck, he opened the passenger door and helped her up into the seat.

Maybe Hank had an alternate location Fin could take Jane until the danger blew over or she remembered who she was and why someone wanted her dead.

Wherever they landed, Fin would be staying with Jane. She might be taking it well, but she needed someone to watch her back. Fin would be there.

THAT NAGGING FEELING of needing to get somewhere fast tugged at Jane. As they left Bozeman behind, she turned and looked over her shoulder. Something about the Montana town was calling to her, lurking in the dark closet of her memory. She just couldn't put her finger on it and draw the knowledge out of the shadows.

Jane sat back in her seat, twisting her fingers in her lap.

"Hopefully, the guy who attacked you in the hospital won't follow us all the way to Eagle Rock and the ranch." Fin sat in the driver's seat of his pickup, his hand resting lightly on the steering wheel. His broad shoulders, straight back and strength gave Jane a sense of security in her world of uncertainty where she didn't know friend from foe.

"I spoke to Hank. He's got his computer guy searching databases for any missing person reports of women meeting your description. He's also going to send someone from his team to search for your vehicle." Fin cast a glance in her direction. "Assuming you were in a vehicle and not tossed from one on the highway where I found you."

"That's good of your friend. I don't know if I can repay him." She curled her fingers into fists. "I don't know if I have money or know where I can get it. How the hell can I pay for the hospital, much less for food, a place to live and transportation? I'm completely at your mercy and reliant on your charity. I hate that. I know, deep down, that I like my independence."

"You can't help what's happening. Hank offers his security services to those who can pay and those who can't. He and Sadie want to give back to their community. They can afford it."

"Still…" Jane glanced out the window, "I don't feel right. Jane doesn't feel like the right name. I don't feel right in my own skin. I want to take action, but I can't."

"You've been in some kind of accident. You have to give your brain and body time to recover."

She pressed her palms to her cheeks, her chest tightening with a sense of impending doom. "I need to remember. It's important and time sensitive."

Fin reached out, took the hand closest to him and squeezed it gently. "Hank and his team are working on it. We'll check in with him and see if they've found anything."

She nodded and held onto his hand. Her lifeline.

In a little less than an hour, Fin drove through the small town of Eagle Rock and back out the other side. A few miles later, he turned off the highway and stopped at a gate with the words "White Oak Ranch" written in wrought iron in an arch over the entrance. He keyed numbers into the keypad, and the gate opened.

After driving through a beautiful stand of ever-green trees, the truck emerged in front of a sprawling stone and cedar home perched on a gently sloping hill with a view of the Crazy Mountains as its backdrop.

A man and woman emerged from the house with a toddler at their heels. The woman had long blond hair and carried a baby on her hip.

Fin smiled at the family. "That's Sadie, my sister, her husband Hank and their children, Emma and McClain." He added in little more than a whisper, "This will be my first time getting to know my niece and nephew."

Jane shot a glance toward him. "How long has it been since you've been here?"

His mouth twisted into a grimace. "I paid a quick visit to see my sister in the hospital in Bozeman after giving birth to her son but, other than late last night, it's been five years since I've been here at the ranch."

"Why did you stay away so long?" Jane asked.

He seemed to chew on his answer for a moment. Jane began to think he would avoid answering altogether.

"Guilt," he said, his tone flat. He didn't elaborate. Instead, he opened his door and dropped down from the truck.

Before he could make it around to her side, Jane slipped out of her seat and eased herself to the ground, not sure her legs were steady enough to support her after sitting for an hour and nearly being suffocated a few short hours earlier.

She was pleased that her legs were strong and held her weight.

Fin cupped her elbow and led her up the porch to stand in front of the beautiful family.

"Sadie, Hank, this is the woman I was telling you about."

Jane held out her hand. "You can call me Jane, for now."

Hank shook her hand and released it. "I'm sorry to hear you've lost your memory."

Sadie handed the baby to Hank then reached out and took Jane's hand in both of hers. Her brow furrowed in concern. "How awful. I can't even imagine how that feels. I think I'd be so scared and…"

"Alone," Jane filled in.

"Exactly." Sadie kept Jane's hand in hers and turned toward the door. "Please. Come inside and have a seat. You're still recovering."

"I'm fine." Jane snorted softly. "Other than not knowing who I am."

"That's bad enough. It's an indication of extreme trauma either physical or mental."

Sadie led her into a massive living room with a stone fireplace that filled one wall and floor-to-ceiling windows with a striking view of the Crazy Mountains.

"Have a seat," she encouraged.

"I'd rather stand for a while after the long drive."

"Then come with me into the kitchen where we can talk." Sadie led the way through the living area into a bright kitchen with everything a chef would want at his fingertips. "What would you like to drink? I have coffee, tea, lemonade and sodas."

"Tea would be nice, thank you."

The little girl raced into the kitchen and skidded to a stop in front of her mother.

"Mama, is that man really my Uncle Fin?"

"Yes, Emma. He is."

She stared up at her mother, her brow wrinkled. "What's an uncle?"

Sadie gave her daughter a smile tinged with a hint of sadness. "He's my brother, which makes him your uncle."

Emma tilted her head. "Mac's my brother. Is he an uncle?"

Sadie laughed. "Not yet, sweetie. When you have children of your own, then Mac will be their uncle."

Emma narrowed her eyes and opened her mouth to argue.

Hank's voice called out before she had a chance. "Emma, come pick up the toys you left on the couch."

Emma darted out of the kitchen as fast as she'd arrived.

Sadie shook her head. "Sometimes, it's hard to explain certain concepts to a four-year-old. Especially since she's never met Fin until now." She filled an electric kettle with water and hit the switch. "I wish he'd come home earlier."

"Does he live somewhere far away?" Jane couldn't help asking.

Sadie shook her head. "Not really. He's stationed at a base near Seattle."

"He's in the military?" Jane asked. That would explain the way he carried himself and the short, tight haircut.

"He is." Sadie laid teacups on a tray and added a couple of coffee mugs. "He joined the Army before Emma was born and hasn't been home since."

Sadie poured coffee from a carafe filled with the steaming brew into the mugs. "I think he blames himself for what happened."

Jane frowned. "What happened?"

Sadie smiled. "Family drama. You don't want to hear about that. We'll scare you off before you've had a chance to get to know us. And it wasn't Fin's fault, anyway. Some people are just crazy, and you don't realize it until they try to burn your house to the ground with you in it."

The glass kettle boiled, taking Sadie's attention.

Jane tried to process what the pretty blonde had said, but none of it made sense. She wanted to ask for further clarification but didn't feel like it was her place to dig into Sadie and Fin's background.

But the questions filled her head.

Who was crazy? Had Fin tried to burn the house to the ground with someone in it? What kind of family was this? They'd appeared so normal when she'd seen them on the front porch.

Sadie poured tea into a teapot, added tea bags and set the pot on the tray. When she had everything where she wanted it, she glanced across the room at Jane. A frown pulled her eyebrows together. "Are you all right, dear?"

Jane shook her head. "I'm fine." She really

wanted to ask if Sadie was all right. She settled on asking something else. "Fin asked me if I knew who Sadie McClain was."

Sadie grinned. "He's always been proud of my success."

"I'm sorry. I don't remember the name Sadie McClain. What do you do?"

"She's only the biggest female movie stars in the country," Fin's deep voice sounded behind her.

Jane spun to face him.

He carried the baby boy in his arms and was grinning at his sister. The baby swatted at Fin's face with a pudgy fist and grabbed for Fin's ear.

Fin took it all in stride, smiling down at the little guy.

The expression on Fin's face as he stared down at the baby melted Jane's heart.

"Mac is going to be a boxer when he gets a little bigger," Fin said and smiled at his sister. "And Emma could easily be a talk show host. Does she ever slow down?"

Sadie laughed. "Never. As soon as Mac learns to walk, he's going to be everywhere. Already, he tries to keep up with his sister by scooting on his belly. He hasn't quite got the hang of crawling."

"It won't be very long. He's a smart guy and

determined to keep up with his big sister." Hank reached out his hands. "Want me to take him?"

"No." Fin held onto the baby. "I've got him. You can have him back when it's time for a diaper change."

"Changed him right before you two arrived." Sadie winked. "He should be good for another minute."

"Swede's in the basement," Hank said. "Want to take our drinks down?"

Fin nodded. "Has he found anything yet?"

Hank shook his head. "Not yet. I sent my guy Kujo and his FBI agent wife, Molly, out to the area where you found Jane. Molly is going to fly her drone along the interstate. Maybe with a bird's eye view, they'll spot Jane's vehicle. Swede tapped into their feed and has the images up on the big screens."

"Great," Fin said.

Hank grabbed the tray of drinks.

"Wait," Sadie added a sippy cup and a bottle of milk to the array with a smile. "Emma and Mac like to be included."

Leading the way, Hank left the kitchen and stepped out into the living area. On a wall was a door that was only visible to someone looking for it. Beside it was a bio scan pad. Hank leaned to one side and let the machine scan his eye.

The door opened, revealing a wide staircase leading into an underground bunker.

"Impressive what you've done with the new house and offices," Fin said.

"Hank's been busy building the business here, and he's setting up satellite offices," Sadie said.

"Already?" Fin grinned. "I'm happy for you, man."

"Got an office now in Colorado and a man in Hawaii. I'm considering setting up an office there and a couple of other places. Word-of-mouth is getting around. There's enough work and former Spec Ops guys leaving active duty to fill the missions." Hank gave Fin the side-eye. "Let me know when you want to come home. I can put you to work for the Brotherhood."

"I, for one, would be thrilled," Sadie said as she poured tea into two cups. She handed one to Jane. "Emma and the baby need their uncle around." She shot him a coaxing smile. "I need you around. We were so close as kids growing up. I miss that."

Jane's heart swelled for the brother and sister. Siblings enriched life. She closed her eyes. How did she know that? Did she have siblings? Were they close? She hated that she couldn't remember someone that important.

Fin looked around the office. "I'll think about it. I'm still not sure I want to come back to Montana. Not after what happened."

Jane's attention zeroed in on Fin. She didn't feel familiar enough with them to ask about what happened. But her curiosity was getting to her.

Hank's lips pressed into a thin line. "It wasn't your fault."

"I should've known something was off. It should never have gone so far."

Sadie touched his arm. "I know you would never have let any harm come to me. You couldn't have known. She was too devious. Hell, I didn't know until it was almost too late."

"But that's all behind us," Hank assured him. "Sadie's alive and well, and we have a good life here on the ranch and in LA when Sadie's on set. We couldn't ask for more."

"Yes, we can," Sadie lifted her chin. "Another baby and for Fin to move home."

Hank's eyebrows rose. "Another baby? Are you...?"

Sadie laughed out loud. "No. I'm not. I have a film to shoot next month. It would be hard to play a jewel thief with a belly." She set her teacup on the conference table and hooked her arm through Hank's elbow. "But I'd like to consider it soon. I want our children to grow up together." She glanced across at Fin. "And I want my brother's kids to grow up with them. Here. On the ranch. The past is in the past. Leave it there."

Fin crossed to his sister, still carrying baby Mac. He leaned over and pressed a kiss to her forehead.

The baby leaned with him and reached for his mother.

Sadie took him in her arms. "I love you, Fin. I want to see you happy."

"Love you, too, Sis. Emma and this little guy are great. I want to get to know them better." He chucked the baby beneath the chin. "I'm glad to see you and Hank are happy here."

A tall, hulk of man with a shock of white-blond hair joined them at the conference table and snagged a cup of coffee. "If you guys are finished making up, you can help me look for Jane Doe's vehicle."

"Sorry, Swede." Hank stepped back. "Swede, this is Fin, Sadie's brother. Army Ranger. Active duty out of Joint Base Lewis-McChord, Washington."

Swede shook hands with Fin. "I won't hold

the Army against you. We've had a couple of Rangers join the team, and they're doing all right."

Fin grinned. "I take it you're a Navy SEAL, like Hank?"

Swede nodded. "Guilty." He held out his hand to Jane. "You must be Jane Doe."

Jane shook his big hand with a firm grip. She wasn't short by female standards, but she had to look way up to meet his gaze. "That's right."

"Sucks to have your hard drive wiped clean, huh?" He let go of her hand and tapped a finger to his temple.

She nodded. "You're Hank's computer guy."

He grinned. "Don't let me confuse you with my geek talk. If I say anything you don't understand, or you have a question about the operations here, just ask. I don't bite."

She smiled up at the big guy. "Thanks." Jane looked over his shoulder at an array of screens on the wall over a desk and at a larger one at the end of the conference table. Images of treetops and mountains passed by on the big screen. "Is that what the drone is broadcasting?"

He turned toward the screen with his coffee cup in one hand. "It is. So far, we haven't spotted anything other than an elk with a huge rack and an old mattress someone dumped off the side of the highway."

Jane moved closer to the screen.

Fin joined her. "Swede can you bring up a map of the highway and give us an approximation of where the drone is in relation to Interstate 90?"

"Got it on one of the small screens." He pointed to the top right monitor that depicted the GPS map of the Interstate highway between Bozeman and Whitehall, Montana. He pointed to a spot on the highway where a blue dot blinked. "This is where the drone is. It's about thirty minutes out of Bozeman."

None of the map or drone images jogged Jane's memory. She studied the drone images.

"Look for shiny metal, shapes that aren't part of nature like straight lines, round wheels. Colors that might not add up to the surroundings. Anything that isn't normal, we zoom in on and check it out."

Fin's eyes narrowed. "I'd just crossed a bridge when I found her. I think it was over a river. I seem to recall seeing a sign with the name of a river on it." He pointed to the map. "There." The blue dot wasn't far from where the river flowed beneath the highway. "Can you have them move to the northwest?"

"I sent them out with a cellphone booster and a satellite phone. I'll try the cellphone first." Hank punched buttons on his cellphone. "Kujo, have Molly take the drone northwest toward the highway bridge crossing the river southeast of Whitehall."

The blue dot moved on the map.

Jane alternated between watching the blue dot on the map and the drone images of the land beneath it. The drone moved over bright green, round patches of farmland where irrigation systems allowed crops to grow on the drier side of the mountains. As the drone moved closer to the river, the patches of green disappeared, and the land dropped off into the river basin. Trees lined the riverside, their canopies blocking the drone's camera from showing what was beneath.

"What's that?" Fin pointed to a spot on the drone screen.

Jane squinted. "What's what? I don't see anything but the top of a tree."

"There." He moved closer. A black crescent barely jutted out of the edge of the green canopy.

"Could be a shadow," Swede said.

Hank spoke into the phone. "Take the drone further north and down on the other side of that stand of trees. Can you see it on your monitor?"

The images grew larger as the drone moved past the tops of the trees and sank lower giving them a better view of what was beneath the tree.

"That's a tire," Fin said.

"People dump tires on the side of the road all the time," Swede said.

"Yeah, but it's not just a tire."

As the drone shifted to the west, sunlight glinted off something shiny next to the black tire.

"That tire is attached to something," Fin said. "It's not a car."

"It's a motorcycle," Swede said.

Hank spoke into his cellphone. "Can you get closer?"

The drone moved closer. As it did, the object became clearer.

The bike lay smashed against the tree, the front twisted at an odd angle, the back tire was what they'd seen first, sticking out from under the branches.

"Can you get to it?" Hank asked Kujo. He hit the speaker button on his phone.

"I'll go down. Molly will stay topside to man the drone," came the male voice on the other end of the call. "It's pretty steep."

Jane's breath caught and held.

Minutes passed with only the sound of Kujo grunting occasionally. Then silence.

"Found it," Kujo said.

"Is there a license plate?" Swede asked.

"Sending a picture of it now," Kujo responded.

Hank's cellphone pinged, announcing an incoming text message. He pulled it up on his screen.

Swede, Fin, Jane and Sadie gathered around. Baby McClain batted at Hank's ear as they all read the numbers and letters on the plate.

"It's an Idaho license plate." Swede spun away. "Send it to me." He dropped into the chair in front of the array of computers and rested his hands on a keyboard, waiting.

Hank forwarded the image to Swede.

As soon as he received it, his fingers flew over the keys.

Everyone gathered around Swede, looking over his shoulder at the screen he flew through. Finally, he stopped on one from the Idaho Department of Motor Vehicles.

The name the plate was registered to was Martin Savage.

Fin turned to Jane. "Does Martin Savage ring a bell?"

She shook her head, straining her thoughts,

reaching into that dark place that refused to reveal her memories. "No."

Swede left the DMV screen up on one monitor and went back to his frenetic keying. A moment later, another image popped up of a man in a business suit. It was an obituary of one Martin Savage from Idaho. The date of death was five days ago in Turkey, where he'd worked with the American Embassy. Murdered by ISIS on his way to work.

"Survived by daughters Aria and Sarah Savage," Sadie read aloud. "Do a search on the daughters."

Swede was already at work sifting through data on the internet to find Aria and Sarah Savage.

"It appears Aria worked as an assistant to her father."

"Any photos of her?" Hank asked.

Swede searched for photographs of Martin and his daughter Aria.

Jane's stomach roiled, and her head spun.

When Swede brought up a screen full of images of Martin Savage at embassy functions, a young, dark-haired woman stood at his side.

Sadie gasped.

Fin shot a glance from Jane to the monitor and back. "It's you."

Swede brought up another image from the

Idaho DMV of a driver's license. The same dark-haired woman stared back at them.

Jane's heart thundered in her chest, and the air around her seemed too thick to breathe.

She had a name.

A fog of darkness swept over her vision. She swayed and would have fallen but for the arm that slipped around her waist and pulled her up against a wall of muscles.

"At least one part of this mystery is solved." Fin smiled gently into her eyes, his strength surrounding her. "Welcome to Montana, Aria Savage."

CHAPTER 6

NOT ONLY HAD he learned the identity of Jane Doe, but Fin also suspected his initial suspicions had just been realized.

Aria Savage, daughter of an employee of the state department working at the American embassy in Turkey, was also the notorious Angel of Death he'd rescued on his mission in Syria a few short weeks earlier.

"If I truly am Aria Savage…" she said, "my father is dead."

"Oh, honey." Sadie touched her arm. "I'm so sorry."

Aria shook her head. "None of this is familiar. Why can't I remember?"

"You were in shock before the accident," Hank said. "I bet crashing the motorcycle and hitting your head pushed you past the shock. Your brain went into self-preservation mode."

"And shut down," Aria said quietly. "But why was I in Montana?"

"I can answer that." Swede nodded toward another screen he'd just popped up.

A young woman smiled for the camera as she signed a paper. The article was about a Coeur d'Alene teen who'd received a full scholarship to attend Montana State University in Bozeman.

Aria frowned. "I was on my way to see my sister." She pushed away from Fin. "I have to get to Bozeman."

"Let Swede locate your sister before we leave," Fin reasoned.

"Whoever tried to kill me might be after Sarah. That had to be why I was in such a hurry to get there."

Fin's brow dipped. "When I picked you up off the highway and said I was taking you to the hospital, you did mention that you didn't want me to take you there because—as you put it—*they'll find me.*"

She met his gaze. "And they did."

"After all this information, are you remembering anything before the accident?" Hank asked.

Aria shook her head and waved at the photo of

her sister. The girl might as well have been a stranger. "I don't remember anything before Fin found me on the highway. I don't even remember riding a motorcycle."

But Fin remembered when she'd ridden a motorcycle into battle and then away once the enemy had been subdued. He recognized her voice, the American accent that had seemed so out of place in Syria, and the kiss she'd given him before she'd ridden into the darkness.

"I need to put the baby down for his nap," Sadie said.

Fin's nephew lay with his head on his mother's shoulder, sucking his thumb, his eyes closed.

Sadie smiled at Aria. "If you'll come with me, I'll find you some clothes. No need to keep wearing the same torn things from your accident."

"I don't need anything. I'm sure I have clothes at my home." Aria looked to Swede. "Could you print out a copy of my driver's license? Surely, it has my home address on it."

"Will do," Swede said. "It shows an address in Coeur d'Alene, Idaho."

"Thank God," she said. "I feel like I'm piecing my life together like a three-thousand-piece puzzle. One that never seems to end."

"At least you have a starting point now," Hank said.

"Aria," Sadie said as if rolling the name around on her tongue. "Much more interesting than Jane. It suits you." She started for the door. "Come on. Let's find you something to wear for your trip back to Bozeman." She called over her shoulder, "Emma, you can come, too."

Emma dragged her feet as she followed her mother up the stairs. "Do I have to take a nap?"

"No," Sadie said. "But you have to brush your teeth and comb your hair. And you can help me find some clothes for Miss Aria."

"Can I?" Emma clapped her hands.

"Yes, ma'am," Sadie said. "After you wash your hands."

Aria cast a glance toward Fin.

"You go ahead." Fin tipped his head toward Sadie and Emma. "I'll be up in a minute. If I know Sadie, she has a closet bursting with everything a woman could want in the way of clothes. People give them to her hoping for her endorsement, and she gets some from the sets of the movies she works on." Fin shook his head. "She can spare a couple of outfits."

Aria followed Sadie and Emma up the stairs.

When the door at the top closed behind them,

Fin turned to Hank. "Aria is more than just the daughter of a statesman."

Hank frowned. "What do you mean?"

"I wasn't sure until now, but I felt like I'd met her before. Now that I know she was in Turkey recently, my instincts were spot on. She was there on the last mission my unit conducted against ISIS in Syria. We rescued a group of schoolgirls ISIS had taken from their classroom."

"Aria Savage was there? A politician's daughter?" Swede's brow twisted. "In Syria? Was she there to teach the girls?"

"No. She wasn't one of the captives. I don't even think she was one of the female fighters who'd participated in the rescue."

Fin explained the situation they'd found themselves in with the machine gunner subduing everything in front of the village gates with a constant barrage of bullets.

"We couldn't leave our positions to make the run out into the open to the limited protection of the village wall. He had complete control. Until a Valkyrie in black drove straight up to the gate, riding a motorcycle. The gunner didn't have enough time to fire on her before she reached the protection of the wall."

Both Swede and Hank looked up simultaneously.

"She rode into live fire. On a motorcycle?" Swede's gaze went to the now empty staircase. "That would go along with her riding a motorcycle when she had her accident."

"Exactly," Fin said, nodding. "She distracted the gunner long enough for my team to scale the wall and get inside."

"But she's a politician's daughter, not a member of the Special Forces," Hank said. "Why would she do that?"

Swede's fingers flew over the keyboard as he queried Aria Savage on several different platforms. There wasn't a lot out there, other than the fact she'd served as her father's assistant in the embassy.

"Who would want her father dead?" Hank asked.

"Looking," Swede said. He spent the next few minutes pouring through the internet pages, reading much faster than Fin could comprehend.

He paused several times to read the details of several articles. When he'd done enough, he raised his head and reported to Hank. "Aria Savage has a degree in political science with an internship working with an Idaho state senator."

"Where did she work after college?" Fin asked.

"She was a staff member for the senator, spending much of her time in Washington DC until she was offered a chance to give back to her country. She went with a group to Turkey, Lebanon and Jordan. When she returned, she quit her job with the senator and joined her father when he was assigned to the embassy in Turkey."

"Where are you getting this stuff?" Fin asked.

Swede grinned. "Got it off her resume stored in the State Department employee database. And," he said, "check this out…she spent a summer training with the Israelis. That makes her a motorcycling mama and a complete badass."

The more Fin learned about Aria, the more he liked her and the more he worried about when her attacker would come back to finish the job.

"I can't find anyone lobbing threats at Martin Savage. He wasn't the Ambassador, but standing with the Ambassador to Turkey, he did his best to help represent the US."

"Could her father's murder have been a random shooting?" Hank asked.

"Not according to the file I'm reading in the State Department's account of the incident. He was stalked and targeted. He was riding with another man he worked with. Martin Savage was killed. The other man was not.

"The shooter tossed a note in through the shattered window." Swede leaned closer to the screen as he read aloud. *"For what you did to my brother, your family will pay."* Swede looked up. "It was signed, Jihadi Jim."

Hank leaned over Swede's shoulder and read the account himself. He turned to Fin. "You're sure it was her on your last mission in Syria?"

Fin nodded, trying to remember everything that had happened in the short amount of time. "We were there to rescue the girls. Intel reported that some of the most violent terrorists had taken them in ISIS. A couple of brothers labeled by the media, Jihadi Jim and Jihadi Joe. To ISIS, they were known as Abu al-Jarah and Abu Sahayb. They were responsible for torturing and beheading at least a dozen people."

"I've heard about them," Hank said. "They captured a Marine Force Recon operator who got separated from his team in one of Syria's bombed-out cities. Before the Marines could extract him, the ISIS brothers tortured him in some of the most heinous ways and then beheaded him on camera. The footage was shared on the Al-Jazeera network."

"While I was trying to get Aria out of range of the gunner and his reinforcements gathering in the streets of the village, one of the ISIS dudes came running out of the walled village. Aria pulled a handgun out of nowhere and dropped the guy before he could kill us." Fin met Hank's gaze. "He was dressed all in black with a black face mask."

Hank nodded. "Like all the media reports of the Jihadi J brothers."

"I didn't think much of it. He was dead. The girls were saved, and we were alive and hustling out of the hot zone. But you know, just before we moved in to take back the girls, a couple of dark SUVs were leaving as we were arriving. One of them could have held the other brother." Fin's eyes narrowed. "Swede, do you think you can access the CIA's files on what happened that night when we rescued those girls? Did they identify the man Aria shot?"

Swede nodded. "They reported that the man was Abu Sahayb, and he'd been shot by an unknown woman who'd arrived on a motorcycle."

"What's out there about Sahayb?" Fin asked.

"He joined ISIS five years ago and worked his way up through the ranks of ISIS fighters. He and his brother spoke perfect English with an American accent. The media latched onto that as they had with Jihadi John back in 2014. Unfortunately, besides an extensive list of people he and his brother tortured and killed, there's not much more to go on."

"American English?" Hank paced the length of the conference table and back. "Why are we fighting our own countrymen?" He stopped to slam his fist on the surface of the table. "I'm tired of losing good men in battles against men of our own country or men using weapons provided by American businessmen, who've never stepped a polished shoe on a battlefield. Please tell me they delivered Sahayb's body to representatives of the CIA."

Swede nodded. "They did, and the investigation determined the body was that of Abu Sahayb, one of the two most wanted terrorists in the Middle East."

"That's it?" Hank clenched his hands into fists. "Damn. That leaves one of the brothers still out there."

"He's not in Syria anymore," Swede said, his lips thinning into a tight line. "Or he's got people in the States doing his dirty work."

Fin's jaw hardened. "Which leaves Aria in danger."

"From what the note said, retribution includes

all of Aria's family," Swede said. "Aria's sister is in danger as well as Aria."

"We have to get to her before the remaining Jihadi J brother gets to her first."

Hank ran his hand over his hair. "If he's already in the States and moving around unnoticed, he was probably some punk kid who'd been on the internet too long, being fed the lies ISIS perpetuates. What started as an online place for a kid to hang out has turned into a recruiting platform to enlist young, angry men willing to fight and die for a country they've never been to or gave a shit about. Brainwashing at its most effective."

"They had to have something deeply wrong with them in the first place," Fin said. "Normal people don't aspire to be terrorists, who behead their enemies and anyone who just plain pisses them off."

"They're probably sociopaths who started their careers killing puppies and kittens for fun." Swede's fingers continued to coax information out of the internet.

He brought up another screen. "This is from the Dark Web. It links the brothers with their monikers Jihadi Jim and Jihadi Joe. When they want to go back to their old lives Stateside, they shed their middle eastern clothes, shave their beards and hop on a plane."

"In other words, they blend in." Fin shook his head. "That's how he was able to slip into the hospital relatively unnoticed. He looked like any other person there to visit a sick relative. He strode right into Aria's room and attempted to smother her to death. No one would've been the wiser if I hadn't caught him in the act."

"Someone needs to stay with her twenty-four-seven," Hank said.

Fin gave Hank a curt nod. "That's my plan." Now, he only had to convince Aria that being with him was her best chance to make it to her next birthday, which she could now deduce based on the printed copy of her driver's license. He picked up the page from the printer. "I'll see she gets this."

"Fin." Hank's voice stopped him before he reached the staircase. "You don't have to do this alone. The Brotherhood Protectors have your six." His serious look turned softer. "And I wasn't kidding. I can use men like you on the team. Think about it."

Fin nodded and hurried up the steps. The door at the top opened automatically, and he stepped into the living room.

The sound of voices came from a room down a long hall.

Moments later, Aria emerged, wearing tailored blue jeans, a pale autumn-yellow sweater, and a brown leather jacket.

The only thing she wore that was hers was the pair of boots she'd worn on the motorcycle.

"Feel better?" Fin asked.

She nodded. "And you weren't kidding about her closet. I've never seen so many unique outfits all in one place."

Fin reached for her hand and raised it to his lips. "You look amazing."

"Not like walking roadkill?" She smiled briefly.

When she did, it made his belly knot and heat burn a path straight to his cock. Now was not the time to get a hard-on. They had to get to Bozeman and find Sarah. The sooner they did, the better.

Aria had lost her father. Fin wasn't sure when or how she'd lost her mother, but her sister was in danger and probably didn't know it. The Angel of Death had suffered sufficient heartache for a long time.

Sadie hurried down the hallway. "Oh, good. I'm glad I caught you. Don't forget to get communications devices and a GPS tracker. And stay with Fin. He can protect you." Sadie drew in a deep breath and let it out. "There. I hope I didn't slow you down by talking too much."

"Not at all," Fin said. "I'm glad you mentioned communications equipment and trackers. I was so bent on catching up with Aria, I forgot Hank had all that stuff." Fin spun toward the hidden doorway in the wall by the stairs.

At that moment, the door opened, and Hank stepped out, carrying a handful of electronics. "Oh, good. You haven't left yet." He held out what he had in his hands. "You might need radios and GPS tracking devices."

Fin tucked the items into his pockets. "Thanks, Hank. You think of everything."

"Not everything," Swede said, having followed Hank out of the basement offices. He held two shoulder holsters packed with handguns. "You two might need these."

Fin took one, and Aria took the other. She shrugged out of the jacket, slipped the shoulder holster into place and slid her arms back into the coat like she'd done it all before.

"Did the Israelis teach you how to handle a gun?" Hank asked.

Aria frowned. "Israelis? I don't know. I wish I could remember. I'm sure there are so many details that would come in handy if only I could access them." She patted the jacket, beneath which lay the loaded gun. "Something feels right about having a gun."

"As long as you know how to use it properly," Fin said.

She gave him a soft smile. "Don't worry. I won't shoot you in the back or anywhere else. I'd rather not use it at all. But it's better to have it and not use than to need it and not have it."

"True," Fin said. "Ready?"

Aria nodded. "Ready."

They left the house, climbed into the truck and headed back the way they'd come.

Fin focused on the road ahead of him, his hands curled tightly around the steering wheel.

He waited until they'd driven through Eagle Rock and were on the open highway to Bozeman before he brought up Syria and the Angel of Death. He explained his experience in his last battle and the woman who'd drawn the attention of the machine gunner, allowing the Rangers to get in and take out the man holding them back from rescuing the schoolgirls.

"That's impressive," she said. "And insane. She drove straight at the gunner? Was she on a suicide mission?"

"No, apparently, she was trying to help. From

what I understand, she'd been aiding the Syrian female fighters in their efforts to take back their homes and lives from ISIS."

"Commendable."

"When I got her away from the village, she thanked me…in English."

Aria raised both eyebrows.

"American English," Fin said, emphasizing American.

"Wow, what's an American woman doing in the Syrian war? Is she part of the Special Forces Command?"

He shook his head. "No. She had long dark hair and dark eyes. And she rode off on her motorcycle before I could get her name. I thought I'd never see her again." He shot a glance her way, taking his focus off the road for a second. "I was wrong."

"Did she show up again?"

He nodded. "She did. On the highway between Whitehall and Bozeman, Montana." Again, he looked her way.

Her brow had furrowed, and her eyes narrowed. "Head injury here…What are you saying?" Then her eyes widened. "You think that woman was me?"

He nodded. "I knew when I found you that you looked familiar, but I couldn't place you. It was like you were out of context for me. I met you on a dusty battlefield in Syria. Then there you were, staggering toward me on a paved highway on the other side of the world. It didn't click until I found out you were with your father in Turkey. Now, it makes sense."

She shook her head. "Makes sense? Nothing makes sense. How could I have been in Syria? Surely, the embassy is a long way from the Syrian border."

"I don't know how you did it, but that woman was you. The man you shot to save me was a known terrorist who got off torturing his victims and beheading them in front of video cameras."

"Then good riddance," she said. "But I still don't remember shooting anyone or driving into machinegun fire."

"The bad news is that man you shot has an equally evil brother. We think the brothers were Americans radicalized to join the ISIS movement in Syria."

"And the surviving brother was the one who left the note in my father's car." She snorted. "So, let me get this right. Not only am I targeted by a killer, but he's also a traitorous bastard who loves to torture his victims. I'm screwed, and you've bitten off a lot more than you bargained for when you rescued me off the highway. I bet you wish you'd just left me there."

"Not actually." He reached for her hand. She laid her fingers in his palm.

He squeezed her hand gently. "There is one other thing that made it hard for me to forget you and that night in Syria."

"Holy hell." She laughed. "There's more?"

He nodded. "Before you rode off on your motorcycle, you kissed me."

CHAPTER 7

BUTTERFLIES FLUTTERED against the inside of Aria's belly at the way Fin's blue eyes darkened when he glanced her way.

Aria already trusted him with her life and her sister's for only having known him for less than twenty-four hours. But it was more than that. She felt like she'd known him a lot longer, and he made her feel things she couldn't remember feeling for any other human. But then she couldn't remember much before waking up in the backseat of his pickup.

She'd kissed him on a battlefield in Syria? What? Was she just crazy?

Aria stole glances at him, her imagination taking her to Syria, where she'd kissed this man. Why couldn't she remember that little detail?

What had it felt like? More than likely, she'd been hopped up on an adrenaline rush. And after he'd gotten her out of the line of fire, she would have been very grateful. But to kiss him?

Her core heated, and her belly tightened. She'd like to repeat the kiss. So that she'd know what it had been like. Had he kissed her back? Did he reject her or wish she hadn't?

The more she looked his way, the more she wanted to repeat the kiss. Purely on the off-chance that it would trigger a memory.

Bullshit.

Her inner conscience called her out on the lie. She found Fin McClain kind, caring, strong and reliable. But mostly, she found him attractive and sexy.

Kissing him would not be a hardship. But he'd said she'd kissed him, not the other way around. Had he remembered the kiss as something he found offensive?

Considering he was still holding her hand, she guessed he hadn't found it offensive.

Her lips curled in a smile.

Fin got them back to Bozeman in less than an hour, breaking every speed limit between Eagle Rock and Bozeman.

Aria used Fin's cellphone to look up the address

of the university. While she was giving him directions that would take them to campus, Fin's phone pinged an incoming text.

She glanced down at the message. "Swede just sent us the address for Sarah's apartment."

Another text came through with an image.

Aria glanced at the picture. "He also sent her class schedule.

"Good," Fin said. "She might be in one of her classes."

"True." Aria stared at the road in front of them. "I hope she'll forgive me for forgetting her."

"I hope you remember her." Fin reached for her hand and held it loosely in his.

She liked how long and slender his fingers were. And so strong.

"No matter who remembers what," her fingers tightened around his, "I can't let what nearly happened to me happen to her."

"Right."

"According to her schedule," Aria glanced at one of the sheets Swede had printed for them, "she should be in College Algebra."

He tipped his head toward his cellphone in her hand. "Could you look up the building and her location?"

"Will do." Aria scrolled through to the university website until she found a map of the buildings on campus and the one her sister had a class in at that moment.

Fin parked his truck in visitors' parking. He rounded the front to help Aria out onto the pavement.

Hand in hand, they approached the building and passed through the double doors to step inside.

A few stray students, either late for their lecture or in between scheduled classes, walked down the hallway toward them.

Aria paused in front of a room, looking down at the page and back up to the numbers on the classroom door. "This is it."

She hesitated for a moment, wondering if she should wait for the class to be over or just barge in and look for Sarah. Aria grabbed the door handle.

Before she could twist the knob, the door burst open. She had to step back quickly to avoid being knocked over.

Students spilled into the hall, hurrying for their next cup of coffee or another class, back-to-back from the first.

When the last person exited the classroom, Aria poked her head through the door. No one remained but the instructor, gathering her books and stuffing them into a large bag.

Aria cleared her throat to get the instructor's attention. "Excuse me."

The instructor, a large woman with warm dark eyes, glanced up. "Can I help you?"

"Hi, I'm Aria Savage, Sarah Savage's older sister. I understand she's one of your students. Have you seen her today?"

The instructor's brow wrinkled. "Is she dark-haired like you?"

Aria nodded.

"She didn't show up for class." The instructor's eyes narrowed. "Sarah usually sits in the front row, and she's always on time."

"Has she missed any other classes with you?"

"No. Just today." Her brow dipped. "Is anything wrong?"

Fin cupped her elbow. She found she needed his presence as much as she needed to breathe. "I don't know," Aria said. "I need to find her to make sure."

"Sorry I couldn't help." The instructor shoved the last book into the satchel and closed the flap. "I hope she's okay."

Aria nodded and left the room with Fin at her side. "Not good," she muttered.

"You don't know that."

"I've been out of commission for an entire day. The attack in the hospital was last night. The man who attacked me could have gotten to my sister last night after he left my room." Aria picked up the pace. "We need to get to her apartment."

"Swede sent the address. I've got it programmed into my map application on my cellphone." As he ran alongside her, he checked his phone. "It's ten minutes away."

When they arrived at his truck, Aria climbed aboard without his assistance.

Fin headed straight for the driver's side slipped in behind the wheel and fired up the engine.

They were out of the parking lot and headed for Sarah's apartment complex, exceeding a few speed limits along the way.

When they arrived at the building, the parking lot was half empty.

Aria studied the license plates of the few vehicles parked there. She pointed to a small red SUV. "There's one from Idaho. It could be my sister's."

"Maybe she stayed home because she didn't feel well," Fin suggested.

Aria had thought of that as well, but her gut was telling her that wasn't the reason why Sarah hadn't shown up for class that day.

Fin parked.

Before he shut off the engine, Aria was out of the vehicle and hurrying toward the building.

"Hey," Fin called out, running to catch up. "What if the guy who attacked you is in the building?"

Aria increased her speed. "Then I need to hurry before he harms my sister."

"You need backup." He darted ahead to enter the building first. "Hell, we both might need backup." He snagged her arm. "Let me go first."

She gave a quick nod, shook free of his grip, and waited for him to pass her and head for the stairwell leading up to the second floor.

Fin took the steps two at a time. When he arrived at the second-floor landing, he didn't have to wait for Aria.

She ran up the stairs on his heels. Her heart pounded against her ribs, not because of the exertion but in hopeful anticipation. If her sister were in her apartment, she'd have at least one person who knew who she was and would know some of the memories Aria no longer had access to. If she wasn't there…

As they arrived in front of the correct apartment, Aria sucked in a deep breath.

Fin raised a hand to knock. When he touched the door with his knuckles, it swung inward.

A young blond-haired woman crouched a few steps away, holding a baseball bat, her eyes wide, frightened. "Take one more step, and I'll pound you."

Fin held up his hands. "We're not here to hurt you."

"Yeah, well, I don't know that. And after what happened to my apartment, I don't trust that you're telling the truth."

Aria leaned past Fin. "I'm Aria Savage, Sarah Savage's sister. Is this her apartment?"

The blonde sucked in a shaky breath. "Yes. We share the apartment. Only she's not here. I just got home a few minutes ago and found the place like this."

Aria's gaze swept the small living room. It looked like a tornado had gone through, leaving everything torn, shredded or flung in all directions.

"We're not going to hurt you, but I'm worried about my sister," Aria reassured the blonde.

"You and me both," the girl said, a sob choking off her words.

"When was the last time you saw her?" Fin asked.

"Last night at the sorority house. We had a sleepover with the members. She must have left early this morning because she had an early class. I slept in and had breakfast at the house. When I came back to the apartment…." Her eyes filled with tears, and she lowered the bat. "I could care less about our things. I just want to know Sarah is okay."

The wail of a siren made the girl shake her head. "That will be the police. I called first thing."

"Do you mind if I look around? I promise not to touch or disturb anything. I'm sure the police will want to dust for prints or something." Aria smiled gently at the woman. "What's your name?"

"Kylie." She stepped back. "You look just like your picture. Sarah talks about you all the time." She pressed her fingers to her lips. "God, I hope she's okay." Tears streamed down her cheeks.

Aria and Fin entered the apartment and surveyed the damage.

Aria wasn't sure what she was looking for. She hoped whoever had done this had left a clue, or that Sarah had somehow left breadcrumbs for them to follow.

Nothing jumped out at her in the living room.

In Sarah's bedroom, the bedding had been

shredded and the mattress appeared to have been stabbed several times with a big knife.

A shiver rippled down Aria's spine. Thankfully, there was no blood on the floor or anywhere else. It gave her a small amount of hope that Sarah was still alive. She prayed she was.

A photo frame lay broken on the floor, empty of the photo.

"That frame held a picture of Sarah, you and your father," Kylie said. "She talked to it every night before she went to bed. I think she was lonely for family. She wasn't going to go to the sleepover, but I talked her into it."

Which might have saved her life. Aria left the bedroom and found Fin in the living room, squatting beside a windup clock lying face-up on the floor.

He looked up. "Kylie, did this clock work?"

Kylie moved around Aria to see what he was looking at. "Yes. We had it in the living room as a reminder of what time it was so we wouldn't be late for class. It's old-fashioned, but it doesn't rely on electricity, and it doesn't have batteries. We wind it up once a week." She frowned. "Is it broken?"

He nodded and met Aria's gaze.

She bent to read the time on the clock's face.

"Three-forty-five. You think that's what time he was here?"

Fin shrugged. "That would be my guess."

"Did you note what time Sarah left the sorority house?" Fin asked Kylie.

Kylie closed her eyes for a moment. "I looked at my smartwatch so I'd know how much longer I could sleep. I think it was a little before five o'clock. Sarah wanted to shower and study before she went to class. She's an early riser." She grimaced. "Not me." Her gaze took in the mess of the apartment. "I should've come back with her. Maybe this wouldn't have happened. You know… safety in numbers and all."

Two police officers arrived at the door to the apartment.

Kylie gave the officers the same information she'd told Fin and Aria. One of them jotted down notes while the other called in a missing and possibly endangered woman report.

Aria found a small photo album lying amid the items strung out across the living room.

"That's Sarah's," Kylie said. "She's been filling it with her favorite photos. I thought it was cute that she went to the trouble of printing photos when everything is online these days."

Aria flipped through the pages, her chest tightening. Many of the images were selfies of Sarah.

She stared at the young woman's face, willing her memories to return. How could she forget growing up with this bright, beautiful girl who smiled with pure, youthful joy?

She removed one of the photos from the book and handed it to the officer taking notes. "This is my sister. Please, help me find her."

He nodded and took the photo from her hand. "We'll do the best we can."

The other officer interjected. "Dispatch put the word out to be on the lookout for her. We'll also canvass the neighborhood and see if anyone noticed a vehicle coming or going between three am and six."

Aria nodded. It was something better than nothing. But it wasn't enough.

Fin gave the officer his phone number. "If you hear anything about Sarah Savage, please call this number. It's the only way you can get in touch with her sister."

"Have Sarah's parents been informed of her disappearance?" the officer asked.

Aria answered. "No. They're dead."

The man dipped his head. "I'm sorry for your loss." He pulled a card out of his uniform pocket and handed it to Aria. "If you come up with any information that might help us find her, don't hesitate to call. In the meantime, you need to leave the apartment to our crime scene investigation team. They'll want to dust for prints."

"Can I get a few things from my room?" Kylie asked.

One of the officers walked her into her room and waited while she grabbed clothes, toiletries and shoes and shoved them into a gym bag.

When she emerged from her bedroom, she hurried over to Aria. "I'm sorry about Sarah. I wish I'd come back with her."

"You couldn't have known," Aria said.

"Are you going to be all right?" Fin asked.

Kylie nodded. "I'm going to stay at the sorority house for a while. I don't think I can sleep in this apartment anymore. Not after..." She shook her head.

Aria and Fin walked her out to her car and watched as she drove away.

The police were still in the apartment, waiting for the crime scene investigators to show up.

Aria looked around the parking lot at a loss. "Where to?"

"I've no clue. Maybe Hank and Swede have

something for us." Fin pulled his phone out of his pocket and called Hank.

Aria only half-listened as Fin filled Hank in on what had happened at Sarah's apartment.

There had to be some clue left behind. But what?

"Hey, lady," a voice said from behind Aria.

She spun and faced a thin, grizzly-bearded man dressed in old dirty clothes and smelling of booze.

"Are you a Miss Aria Savage?"

She nodded, her muscles bunching in a fight-or-flight reaction at being approached by a stranger. Hell, everyone was a stranger, and she couldn't tell who was friendly or out to kill her.

"Yes," she answered hesitantly.

He held out something. "This is yours."

Her hand came up automatically, and the man dropped a cellphone into her palm.

"This isn't mine," she said, staring at the device.

He shrugged and started to turn. "He said you'd say that. I don't give a rat's ass. I got a G-note for delivering it. I did my part."

"Wait." Fin joined Aria. "Who gave you the phone?"

Again, the man shrugged. "Some dude dressed in black like some ninja or burglar. Look, I didn't steal the phone. I'm just the delivery guy. You have questions, take it up with the ninja."

"Where can I find him?" Aria asked.

"Hell, if I know. He handed me the phone and the money and split."

"You could've walked away with both," Fin noted.

The man's mouth quirked up on one side. "Thought about that but didn't want anyone to come looking for me and slit my throat in the night. Got enough of those types lurking in the shadows, willing to kill ya for your shoes, much less for a cellphone." He shook his head. "No thanks. I earned my pay, and I'm outta here."

"Did you see if he got into a car?" Aria asked.

"Nope. Once he handed me the hundred, I didn't see anything else. Doesn't pay to be too nosy."

Short of grabbing the guy and shaking answers out of him, Aria and Fin couldn't keep him from leaving.

Aria stared at the phone in her palm.

"It's a burner phone," Fin said.

"Should we hand it over to the police and let them dust it for prints?" she asked.

"I'm betting if he went to the trouble of giving

you a burner phone, he wiped it clean before handing it to the homeless guy."

Aria continued to stare at the phone, waiting for it to ring. A minute passed, then two.

Fin's gaze swept the parking lot and the roofs of the surrounding buildings. Then he cupped her elbow, bringing her close to him. "Come on. We can wait in the truck. I don't like being out in the open...exposed."

She let him lead her to the passenger side of his pickup and help her up into the seat, her attention on the device in her hand.

"He has Sarah," she said. It wasn't a question.

Fin's lips pressed together in a thin line. "Most likely."

Aria looked up from the phone, her gaze meeting his. "But he wants me, too."

"I'd say so."

"And this is how he'll get me." She glanced back down at the burner phone. "He'll use Sarah to get me to come to him."

"Thus, the phone," Fin agreed.

She let out a hard sigh. "Then he'll kill us both."

His jaw hardened. "That's not happening on my watch."

"*I* won't let that happen. Not to my sister,

anyway." Her eyebrows descended. "If he harms one hair on her head, I'll…I'll…."

He took her empty hand in his. "We won't let that happen."

She prayed he was right and that they could stop a maniac.

The burner phone in her hand represented a lifeline to her sister, at the same time as it connected them with a homicidal lunatic.

CHAPTER 8

As DAYLIGHT WANED and darkness settled over Bozeman, Fin was ready to punch someone. The stress of waiting was killing him.

And it wasn't helping Aria, either. She'd spent the day jumping at any sound, expecting the burner phone to ring at any minute. When it hadn't, she'd worried that it wasn't working and called Fin so that he could return the call to the burner phone number.

It worked fine.

Fin could imagine all the horrors racing through Aria's mind. They were going through his as well.

Jihadi Jim could be torturing her sister as they sat waiting for a call that wouldn't come in time to save her.

They'd spent the day sitting in the truck, sometimes driving around Bozeman, hoping to catch a
glimpse of Jihadi Jim, even though they didn't
know what he looked like.

Hank kept him up to date with what they were
doing back at the ranch. He had Swede tap into the
hospital's computer system to look at the videos of
people coming and going from the hospital around
the time Aria had been attacked. Several men were
of the same height and build who'd attacked Aria.
They were wearing dark pants and shirts and had
entered the hospital through the Emergency
Department.

Swede was able to weed out most of them by
the timestamps on the records created by the
administrative staff and nurses. He'd crosschecked
their names with the DMV and state and federal
criminal databases. He'd gotten no hits on those
who'd given their names.

"But that doesn't account for the one or two of
them who either came in to be with someone else
or came in to attack Aria," Hank said. "Swede's
running facial recognition software with the
images he was able to capture. It's a slower
process. We'll let you know if we find anything
useful."

That had been a couple of hours earlier.

Tired of being cooped up in the truck, Fin drove toward the interstate. "What do you say about grabbing some pizza and finding a hotel room to hang out in?"

Aria's eyes widened.

"What? Don't look at me that way." Fin grinned. "I need a shower and to move around."

She nodded. "I'm tired of sitting, too, and pizza sounds good."

When he pulled up in front of a hotel, Fin could see Aria stiffen beside him.

"Look, I'm not planning to take advantage of you. I just need a place to shower, change and stretch. Nothing else." He met her gaze. "Or we stay in the truck for who knows how much longer. I'll be okay either way."

Aria drew in a deep breath and let it out slowly. "I need to stretch. Get a room. We'll hang out until we get the call." She glared at the burner phone. "Why isn't he calling? You'd think he'd want to get this over with, sooner rather than later."

"His mind might not work that way. He could be delaying your reunion with your sister as a method of torturing you."

Aria closed her eyes, her face tight, her lips pressed into a flat line. "Bastard."

"Yes, he is." Fin waited until she opened her

eyes and looked into his. "Room or not?"

She dipped her head once. "Room."

He got out of the truck and rounded the front to her side.

When he opened the door, she frowned. "I can wait here."

"The hell you can. I'm not letting you out of my sight. Especially while you're out in the open." He held out his hand.

She placed hers in his and allowed him to help her to the ground. Her heel caught on the running board, and she pitched forward, crashing into his chest.

Fin caught her easily, wrapping his arms around her waist, steadying her until she had both feet firmly planted. Even then, he didn't let go. He liked how soft and warm she was pressed against his body.

He gazed into her eyes, memorizing the flecks of gold in the dark brown of her irises. "At night, when I lay in my Army cot, I could still see the starlight reflected in your eyes."

Her brow wrinkled. "Really?"

He nodded. "You made an impression on me."

"Based on what you said about the incident, we were only together for maybe five or ten minutes?"

"Those five or ten minutes were unforgettable.

We watched you ride into the fray like a badass superhero. It wasn't until I was sent in to retrieve you that we realized you were a woman. That sent you up several notches on the scale of badassery."

"It couldn't have been me," she said, staring up into his eyes. "Surely, I would remember kissing you."

He chuckled. "I must not have made much of an impression."

Aria frowned. "It's this damned amnesia. I know there must be so many memories that mean a lot to me. I just can't get to them."

"Do you realize that your courage and selflessness made me reevaluate my own actions. I had been so bent on taking on the most dangerous tasks and missions, I wasn't thinking about the rest of my team and the consequences of my recklessness. I think I was punishing myself for what happened in my past instead of letting go of the past. And you made me think about my family and the fact that I hadn't been home in five years. You put yourself at risk for strangers. Women who had no other choice but to take up arms to secure their homes and families."

He shook his head, a sad smile curving his lips. "I squandered five years I could've spent getting to know my niece, nephew and brother-in-law. All because I was embarrassed that I hadn't seen the evil in one person until it was almost too late."

Aria cupped his cheek and gave him a crooked smile. "All of that because of one kiss?"

His heart swelled. She'd been through hell and was worried about her sister, but she still cared about others and tried to make him smile.

"The old me could easily fall in love with you," he whispered.

Her eyes flared, and then she shifted her gaze to somewhere in the middle of his chest. "The old you?"

His jaw hardened, and he stepped back. "Don't worry. I've vowed never to fall in love again. Apparently, I'm not good at it."

Her head shot up, and she met his gaze in challenge. "Why do you say that?"

"It's a long story and has to do with the past I need to leave behind," he said. "We should go inside and get a room before they're sold out."

Aria slipped her hand into his as they stepped through the automatic sliding doors into the lobby.

He almost pushed her hand away but didn't. He liked holding it. Too much. But he couldn't allow himself to get too close to her or any other woman. Not after Carla. He didn't trust himself to know the difference between someone loving him and someone pretending to love him. If he was the only one at risk, he might not be so careful. But he wasn't the only one involved. He had a rich and famous sister, with a great husband and two precious children to think about. He'd never put them in danger. Not again.

WHILE FIN SECURED A ROOM, Aria walked around the lobby, checking out the coffee bar set up for the guests to help themselves. If they didn't have any in the room, she might come down later for hot water and tea.

Her pulse had kicked up the moment they'd stepped into the building. It was one thing to be alone in the cab of a pickup with a man she'd only known for twenty-four hours. It was entirely different being alone with a stranger in a hotel room.

Though, she didn't think of Fin as a stranger. After discovering she had no memories, he was the first person she'd connected with in her new normal. He was the first person who had shown her kindness and had taken the time to make sure she was all right. He hadn't abandoned her at the hospital as she'd expected him to.

Fin had gone out of his way to help her, even fighting off her attacker and getting his family to help her figure out who she was.

And they hadn't stopped there. Hank and his team were actively searching for the man who had attacked her and most likely had kidnapped her sister.

They could have left her in the hands of the local police and let them search for her sister. Instead, Fin had urged Hank and Swede to take her on as a client, owning her problem, instead of brushing her off for someone else to deal with.

She had no one else. With or without her memories, she was on her own to find her sister. Fin and the Brotherhood Protectors had stepped up to the task of protecting her and finding Sarah.

"Ready?"

Aria jumped.

Fin stood behind her with a crooked smile. "I didn't mean to scare you." He held up a room key card. "This one is yours. I got two rooms."

She took it, frowning. "I thought you didn't want me out of your sight."

"I don't. Our rooms are adjoining. We can keep the door open between us. I didn't want you to feel uncomfortable."

"But that's two rooms. I already owe you so

much for taking me in." She handed the key back to him. "Cancel the room. We can share. It's not like I'm going to sleep tonight." She held up the burner phone.

"Me either." His lips twisted. "Are you sure?"

"I am. Besides, maybe I don't want to be in another room."

Fin chuckled. "Was I reading you wrong?"

Aria shrugged. "No. It's just that everything is moving so fast. I don't have time to absorb what's going on around me and how I feel about it."

He held up the card key. "I'm taking it back. I got a room with two queen-size beds. You can have one all to yourself, and I'll be in the room with you. I can also hide all of the pillows if you want me to," he said softly, not so much as a joke.

Aria smiled. "It's okay. As I said, I don't think I could sleep. Not knowing when we'll get the call will keep me on edge."

"Okay then, I'll cancel the second room." He turned toward the reception desk.

"Fin?" Aria called out.

He performed a perfect about-face. "Yes, ma'am."

"Thank you for being so considerate when you didn't have to be."

"I saved you. I'm responsible for you." He winked. "I'll be right back."

Aria studied him as he spoke with the clerk who canceled the room and reversed the charges.

"I need to park the truck. Are you—"

"—coming with you?" she finished for him. "Yes."

Together, they left the lobby and climbed into the truck.

Fin parked it beneath a light, grabbed a gym bag and slid out of the driver's seat onto the ground. He rounded the truck to open the door for Aria.

She couldn't help thinking that she could get used to the way he pampered her, anticipating her needs.

Aria got out and met him at the tailgate.

As they walked back into the hotel, she slid her hand in his, loving how safe he made her feel.

But safe wasn't the only thing she felt.

She was nervous, excited and...hot...in places she shouldn't be feeling hot with a man she had kissed on a battlefield and known for maybe a day. She chastised herself for her lusty desires, glad that the man generating them couldn't read her mind.

Her concern in sharing a room had not been

because she didn't trust him. She didn't trust herself.

Their room was on the second floor.

"Do you mind if we take the stairs?" Fin asked.

"Not at all. I prefer stairs when I don't have to go up fifty flights."

Fin chuckled as they climbed the steps. "Fifty's your limit?"

Aria laughed as she reached the landing on the second floor. "Maybe one floor is my limit, especially if I'm carrying ten bags of groceries."

They arrived in front of the door to their room.

Fin waved the key card over the locking mechanism. A green light blinked. He turned the handle and pushed the door open.

Inside, the room had recently been updated with new wall coverings, furniture and carpet. The bathroom had been redesigned with more modern décor, everything clean and shiny.

Aria eyed the queen beds, and a shiver of excitement rippled through her.

Fin stood inside the room, his back to her. "You choose where you want to sit. I need a shower. If anything happens while I'm underwater, let me know immediately."

Aria nodded, her mouth going dry over the thought of barging into the bathroom where Fin would be naked, water dripping from every part of his body.

She licked her lips and stepped away before she did something stupid like kissing him again.

Kissing him in Syria was different. She'd probably figured she'd never see him again. That would have been exciting. Coupled with the adrenaline of a headlong charge into the fray had to have been a complete rush. It was only natural to kiss the man who'd saved her.

Damn, she wished she could remember.

Fin reached into his pocket and brought out a plastic bag of toiletries. "I picked these up at the desk."

She took the offering like it was the most precious gift he could have given her. And for everything that had happened in the past twenty-four hours, a toothbrush and toothpaste sounded like heaven. Brushing her teeth wasn't something she had to remember how to do. It came naturally, like brushing her hair.

Fin dug in the other pocket and pulled out a comb. He handed it to her with a grimace. "Sorry, they didn't have a brush."

She smiled. "A comb is fine. Thank you for thinking of these."

"Do you want to make use of the bathroom

first?" he asked.

She shook her head. "No. I had the pleasure of showering in the hospital. I can wait a few more minutes."

Fin crossed to the door and twisted the deadbolt. "I'll order pizza when I get out. If someone knocks on the door, don't open it. If the place is on fire, let me know first. Don't open the door."

She gave him a grin and mock salute. "Yes, sir."

He chucked her beneath the chin. "And if the phone finally rings, get me out of the shower. I want to hear what he has to say."

Her smile faded, and she nodded.

Fin entered the bathroom and closed the door. After he'd used the facilities and flushed, he opened the door a crack and looked around the edge. "You okay?"

She nodded, her cheeks burning when she realized she'd been caught staring at the bathroom door.

"If you need me, just yell." He left the door ajar.

A moment later she could hear the sound of water and the squeak of metal on metal as he moved the shower curtain.

Aria could imagine him standing naked beneath the spray, water running in rivulets over his body.

She licked her lips as if she were licking the moisture from his skin. Her pulse raced, and heat built low in her belly.

For a moment, she set the burner phone on her bed, flexing her fingers. They were cramping from holding the device for the last few hours.

It wouldn't hurt for her to set it down for a few minutes. She wasn't going to leave it in the room while she explored the hotel. She didn't care about exploring what the hotel had to offer. They were only there until they got the call from her sister's captor. Then the negotiations would begin.

Her life for her sister's.

Her sister's life for letting the bastard walk away without being pounded into oblivion.

Aria paced to the window and back to the door, slowing as she passed the slightly open doorway to the bathroom where a naked Fin would be rubbing soap over his skin.

Did he need help getting those hard-to-reach places?

Aria reached out her hand, ready to push the door open wider and ask.

She caught herself before the door moved and let her hands fall to her sides. She leaned her back against the wall beside the door and closed her eyes, letting her imagination take her through the door and into the shower with Fin. She'd rub soap all over his body, rinse and repeat, slowing as she grazed her fingers over the poker hard thickness of his shaft.

Her hands would wrap around him and slide from tip to base and back. Again. And again.

Aria raised her hand to her breast. The tip of her nipple had puckered into a hard little bead, ready for his lips to claim.

She moaned before she could stop herself and her core flamed, sending a wash of cream through her channel.

Aria tweaked her nipple between her thumb and forefinger, rolling it, tugging on it and wishing it was Fin's mouth claiming her there. And lower.

As the water sprayed the man in the other room, Aria's fantasy continued.

She splayed her other hand over her torso, sliding it downward and into the waistband of the jeans Sadie had given her. Her fingers continued downward, dipping beneath the elastic band of the thong panties Sadie had pulled from a new unopened package.

Slipping between her folds, she touched herself there and gasped.

A hundred bolts of lightning shot out across her nerves, sending tingling sensations rippling through her body, spreading to the very tips of her ears and toes.

She bit down on her lip to keep from moaning a second time and stroked herself again.

Her breathing grew ragged, and her knees weakened. If she was as turned on by her imagination, she could only imagine how she'd feel if Fin's hands and mouth were really on her.

The water shut off, and the grommets on the shower curtain squeaked as the curtain was pulled to the side.

If she flung open the door, she'd see Fin standing there in all his glory, dripping and naked.

The door swung open and Fin's head poked out, turned toward the beds. "Aria?"

She jerked her hand out of her pants and straightened. "I'm here."

He turned his head in her direction and let out a whoosh of air. "Shit. I thought you were gone."

His face was so close, she could reach out and kiss him like he'd said she'd boldly done in Syria with bullets flying all around. All she had to do was lean forward a few inches and she'd learn what she'd forgotten. Just a few short inches.

Aria swayed toward him, her hand rising to cup his cheek. She closed the distance, and her lips connected with his. Lightly at first. As if she needed to test the waters. Was he receptive? Would he think she was too forward or needy? Would he reject her and everything between them become awkward?

The feathery soft feeling of his lips on hers made her want more. She turned and pressed her body to his damp one and increased the pressure, sliding her tongue along the seam of his lips until he opened to her.

Then all bets were off as she pushed past his teeth and claimed his tongue, sliding hers along the length of his, tasting him in a sensual dance.

His hands came up to her hips, pulling her closer, the hard evidence of his desire pressing into her belly.

Aria was on fire, her body burning to be with Fin. Skin to skin. Naked and connected in the most intimate way.

Pushing her hands between them, she fumbled with the buttons on her blouse, loosening a few before she gave up and pulled the garment over her head, tossing it to the side.

Fin mastered the button on her jeans, freeing it from its anchor and drawing the tab of the zipper downward.

In a frenzy to be free, Aria pushed the jeans

down her legs, toed off her boots and kicked the jeans to the side.

Standing in the thong panties and a lacy black bra, she stared up into Fin's blue eyes, her breathing ragged, her heart racing. "Tell me you don't want this, and I'll stop now."

He chuckled. "Isn't that my line?"

She shook her head. "If it's too fast, I can wait." Her head fell back, and she moaned softly. "Fuck that, I can't wait." She met his gaze. "Make love to me. Just this once. I won't make demands. No strings. No promises. Just sex." She laid her hand on his chest and felt his heart pounding against her fingertips. "Please."

He shook his head, and she nearly died right there.

"You're a strange one," he said. "I feel like I'm holding two women. Jane Doe and Aria Savage." He captured her hand in his and raised it to his lips where he kissed the tips of her fingers, one at a time.

"And I don't know who I am," she whispered. "Sometimes, I think I liked being Jane Doe. At others, I'm glad I have a past, even if I don't remember it." She brought his hand to her lips. "But I feel best when I'm with you."

"Are you sure you're up to this? I don't want to

further injure you." He brushed his lips across her forehead.

"I'm sure." She placed his hand on her breast and reached behind her back to release the clasp on her bra.

Fin pushed aside the fabric and captured her nipple between his teeth, gently rolling the beaded tip. Then he straightened.

Aria frowned. "What's wrong?"

"Not a damn thing," he said. He ducked into the bathroom and came back out carrying a foil package. He handed it to her. "We can be crazy, but not stupid." Fin bent and scooped her up in his arms and carried her to the nearest bed.

Aria cast an eye toward the burner phone and pushed it from her mind. She'd focused on it all day, and it hadn't done a damn bit of good.

Making love with Fin would take her mind off the interminable wait and thoughts of what might be happening to her sister.

Who was she trying to kid? Aria wanted Fin. All of him. Beside her, wrapping her in his arms. On her, kissing, licking and nibbling every inch of her body. And in her, filling her with his thick shaft, thrusting, pumping and reminding her she was alive. Though she'd lost her memories, she could start with Fin, making new ones.

CHAPTER 9

FIN TOOK HIS TIME, learning every curve and crevice of Aria's body, one kiss, one touch and one nibble at a time. Her skin was soft and sweet, and her moans made him so hard he could barely control himself.

But he did. He wanted to bring her to the very edge and over it, finding her release before he mastered his own. If bringing her to orgasm was enough for her, he'd be satisfied.

Well, almost. His cock, already rock-hard, throbbed with his need to be inside her, thrusting into her slick channel.

He'd get there, but not until she got there first.

Trailing his lips across hers, he deepened the kiss.

She opened to him, letting him glide his tongue

along the length of hers, caressing and tasting until he had to move on, anxious to see how she responded to his caresses.

As he kissed a path along her jaw and down the smooth length of her throat, his fingers traced the curve of her shoulder, across her collarbone and down to the swell of her breasts. He pinched the tip, pulling gently.

Aria's back arched off the mattress. She dug her fingers into his hair and guided him lower to replace his fingers with his lips.

He sucked on her tit, drawing it deep into his mouth where he laved the rigid little bead with his tongue, teasing and flicking it until Aria writhed beneath him.

Moving to the other breast, he paid equal attention, massaging it with his hand while tonguing the tip until the nipple contracted to match the first.

With her fingers digging softly into his scalp, Aria guided him lower, crossing the length of her torso.

He moved slowly, savoring the feel of her silky skin against his lips. When he reached the triangle of silk over her sex, he hooked his thumb in the elastic band and dragged the scrap over her thighs and down to her ankles.

She kicked her panties free, letting her knees fall to the side, giving him room to settle his body between her legs.

He moved in, draped her knees over his shoulders and kissed a path along the sensitive skin of her inner thighs. When he reached the apex, he parted her folds with his thumbs and flicked the nubbin at the top with the tip of his tongue.

Aria gasped and dug her heels into the mattress.

The next flick made her moan and lift her hips, urging him to take more.

Loving the way her body responded to him, Fin settled into the task of making her come apart.

He flicked and swirled on her clit until she squirmed beneath him, murmuring his name, begging him not to stop.

While he worked her clit with his mouth, his fingers teased her damp entrance. He pushed one digit inside.

Her channel was slick with the juices of her desire, ready to take him. He was ready, but she wasn't quite there.

Fin sucked her clit and slid three fingers into her channel at the same time.

Aria raised her hips, her fingernails digging into Fin's scalp. Her body stiffened beneath him. With her heels planted in the mattress and her hips raised, her body shuddered and then rocked with her release.

She threw back her head and uttered, "Yes. Oh, yes."

Fin continued to ply her clit with enough stimulus to allow her to ride the wave of her orgasm for several minutes before her hips lowered to the mattress, and she lay limp against the sheets.

She tugged his hair. "Inside me. Now."

He chuckled at her demand. "Yes, ma'am."

After one last taste of her, Fin climbed up her body and settled between her parted legs, his cock nudging her slick entrance.

Aria fumbled for the condom that she'd dropped amid her orgasm. Once she had it in hand, she tore it open and rolled it down over his stiff shaft. Then she guided him to her entrance.

He paused there, the tip of his dick nudging her.

"More?" he asked, not knowing how he'd stop if she declined. His cock was so hard by now that he could drive nails into concrete with it.

"Oh, God, yes." She dug her fingers into his buttocks and brought him to her.

He hesitated with the tip of his cock touching her there.

Her hands tightened on his hips, and her fingernails dug into his buttocks. When Fin started to pull back, Aria increased pressure on his hips, keeping him close. She poked a finger into Fin's chest. "Stop teasing me, and fuck me like there's no tomorrow."

Fin laughed out loud and slid into her channel, gliding slowly until he'd gone as far as he could. He gave her body sufficient time to adjust to his girth before he started moving in and out.

She set the pace by with her hands on his hips. When he had it right, she dropped her hands to her sides and gripped the comforter.

With her tight pussy wrapped around him, it didn't take long for Fin to catapult into the stratosphere. He continued moving inside her, riding the wave of his release until he washed ashore, fully satisfied and ready for more.

After his cock stopped throbbing, Fin pulled free of Aria's warm, wet channel, dropped down beside her and spooned her from behind.

Nuzzling the back of her neck, he whispered, "That was amazing."

She sighed and wrapped his arms around her, bringing one of his hands up to cup her breast. "Yes. It was."

"What if I don't want this to be just once?" he asked, nibbling at her earlobe.

"I'm game to do it again." She turned her head to look back at him. "But are you ready?"

He laughed and squeezed her tight. "No, I'm not ready now, but I will be."

"Mmm." She settled back in his arms and rubbed her ass against his still hard cock. "Let me know when."

He smacked her bare bottom, the sound louder than any pain it caused.

"Hey. Save the spankings for next time," she said. "It's only a tease if you don't follow through."

"You're a mouthy thing in bed."

"You have no idea," she said in a low sultry tone. "Again...let me know when you're ready. I'll show you mouthy."

His cocked twitched. "I'm ready."

She laughed and rolled over in his arms to look into his eyes. "Why is it I don't feel awkward lying naked with you when we've only known each other a very short time?" She kissed him and pulled his bottom lip between her teeth to nibble on it before letting it go.

"We've known each other for several weeks. You might not remember, but we've met before."

She cupped his cheek and brushed her thumb

over his mouth. "I want to remember," she said. "I really do. I want to remember what went through my mind to kiss a soldier and then leave before I got his name."

"I kicked myself for weeks, wishing I'd ask you for yours." He turned his face into her hand and pressed a kiss to her palm. "Your name didn't matter, other than for a way to find you. I was attracted to you, not your name."

"I can't believe you remembered that random kiss."

"It stayed with me as if etched into my mind. And when I found you on the highway, it happened again. I didn't need to know your name. Jane Doe or Aria Savage... Even when you didn't know your real name, I knew who you were where it counts." He touched a hand to her chest.

"So, where does that leave us?"

she asked. "It's too soon to make lasting promises."

"I agree, but I would like to see you again."

She smiled. "You're seeing me now."

He reached up and tweaked her nipple. "You know what I mean. I'd like to get to know you better."

She snorted. "You and me both."

"Will you?"

"Go out with you?" She nodded. "Yes. Absolutely." Her brow furrowed. "But I have to admit, I'm going to be a bit boring. I have no memories of my life experiences. I'll have very little to talk about."

"We'll work on that. Every day comes with new paths to follow and the beauty of the present to experience."

"That's what I keep telling myself. I can't dwell on the past I've lost. I have to live in the present and plan for the future because it'll happen. Whether I plan for it or not."

Fin grinned. "Look at us waxing poetic and shit."

Aria stared into Fin's eyes for a long moment.

"What?" he asked.

"Nothing," she said. "Well, not nothing to me. You have an entire brain to stretch and challenge. I'm committing this moment with you to my memory." She smiled. "Thank you."

Fin's chest tightened. He loved that she was committing their lovemaking to memory. He wished the rest of her memories would come back and make her happy.

ARIA LAY in the warmth of Fin's arms. He'd moved the burner phone to the nightstand beside the bed so she wouldn't have to reach so far to answer it.

She must have drifted off.

A nagging alarm kept going off, jerking her out of her sleep. It wasn't until the third ring that it struck her.

The burner phone.

Damn, damn, damn.

Instantly awake, Aria rolled over, snagged the burner phone and hit the receive button. "Hello."

Fin sat up beside her and leaned close to where she held the phone to her ear.

"2255 South Cherry Street. Exactly one hour from now. For every person you bring with you, your sister will lose a finger. For each minute past the hour, I hit sweet Sarah with thirty volts of electricity. Involve the police...she dies. It's your call."

"How do I know you have her and that she's alive?" Aria's body trembled. The hand holding the phone shook so much she was afraid she'd drop it.

Silence stretched for an interminably long moment.

Aria thought Jihadi Jim had ended the call.

Then she heard a woman cry out in pain.

"Ari?" a scared voice sounded in her ear. "Ari, don't come after me. He's insane. He's going to kill—"

"Sarah!" Aria cried into the phone, but the call had ended.

Tears welled in Aria's eyes. She dropped the phone on the bed and buried her face in her hands. "She's alive."

Fin grabbed his cellphone and punched buttons. "Hank. We have less than one hour to get ready. Do you have access to air transport to get you to Bozeman before then?" He nodded. "Okay. We'll meet you at the Bozeman airport in forty minutes. Get there earlier if you can. We'll be waiting." He ended the call and slipped an arm around Aria. "Focus on the fact Sarah's alive."

"I'm trying," she said. "But you and I know what kind of lunatic this guy is. He gets off on torture. He won't be satisfied until he gets his pound of flesh."

"Focus on the fact your sister is alive. We're going to get her out that way."

Aria shook her head. "You can't. If he finds out you and Hank's team are my backups, he'll follow through on his promise." She swallowed hard on the lump in her throat. "Can't let that happen."

"We'll figure it out."

Still shaking, Aria allowed herself a few more minutes in the warmth of Fin's arms. Then she turned, kissed him full on the lips and pressed her forehead to his. "In case something happens to me, I want you to know how much our time together has meant to me."

"Sweetheart, it's not over yet. We're going to be seeing a lot more of each other." He reached for her hand and squeezed it before releasing her.

Aria slid off the bed and went through the room, searching for the clothes Sadie had given her. When she had them all gathered, she dropped them on the bed and started pulling them on. "I know what I'm getting into. If Jihadi Jim has his way, neither my sister nor I will come out alive. Promise me that if it comes to a choice between saving Sarah or me, save Sarah. She deserves a long, beautiful life."

Fin swung his legs out of bed and stood. "And you don't?" He grabbed his pants and stepped into them.

"I've had more years than she has. And I brought this issue with Jihadi Jim to my family by my careless involvement in a war I had no business getting into the middle of. It's already cost my father his life. I won't let anyone kill my sister as if her life doesn't matter."

"The Jihadi brothers had no business being in Syria, either," Fin pointed out. "But they did get involved and built a legacy of terror."

"Yeah, now one of them is back and wants to practice his skills on my sister." Aria's fists clenched. "It can't happen."

"Based on everything my sister has told me about the Brotherhood Protectors, I believe Hank will come through."

"And if he doesn't, I need to be prepared to fight my way out and free my sister."

Aria glanced at the clock on the nightstand. "We now have fifty minutes remaining." She pulled her blouse over her head and buttoned it. After pulling on her jeans, she stepped into her boots and pulled the tangles from her hair using the comb.

Fin was ready before her and waiting beside the door with their things packed inside his pathetically small gym bag. When they had Sarah back, and things were back to some semblance of normalcy, he'd take Aria shopping for new clothes, or he'd drive her over to Coeur d'Alene to her old house where she could collect what she needed.

Hell, she might want to stay in Coeur d'Alene. Not that Fin had any say about it.

He had to go back on active duty. His two weeks of leave would soon come to an end. He wouldn't get back to Idaho or Montana for a long time.

Pushing all the negative thoughts from his mind, he focused on the task ahead. They had to keep Aria alive and free Sarah.

Fin and Aria left the hotel and drove to the Bozeman Regional Airport. Already twenty-five minutes of the allotted hour had passed.

Aria sat in the passenger seat of Fin's pickup, staring out at the runway. As late as it was, no planes were flying in or out.

Fin reached across the console and took her hand in his. "It's going to work out. It has to. We aren't done, you and me." He stared into her dark eyes. "What were the odds that we'd run into each other in Syria and then again in Montana? I truly believe we were meant to be together. We can't fight it, and we shouldn't."

Her lips quirked. "What about your vow never to fall in love again? You never did tell me why."

"It's a long story," he said, turning to stare out at the runway.

"I'd like the CliffsNotes version," she said. "I don't want to die without hearing it."

His brow dipped low, and he squeezed her hand. "You're not going to die."

"And you're avoiding the subject." She cocked an eyebrow in challenge.

Fin sighed. "Okay. Here it is in a nutshell."

Taking a deep breath, he launched into the story. "My sister was being stalked and threatened. She thought she'd be safe out at the ranch, but the threats became more serious. Hank, her high school sweetheart, came home from his stint as a Navy SEAL medically retired. He stepped in to protect her. At the time, my wife, Carla, and I lived at the ranch. I didn't know until almost too late that the threats were coming from my wife. You see, Carla was jealous of Sadie's success. She couldn't have Sadie's life, but she could have her ranch. All she had to do was stage an accident that would kill Sadie."

Aria shook her head. "How could anyone want to hurt your sister? She's about the nicest person I've met."

"Seriously. But then Carla was a crazy bitch bent on knocking Sadie out of the picture so we could claim full ownership of the ranch. Eventually, she planned to feed me poisonous mushrooms or bash me in the head and make it look like an accident. She wanted the ranch all to herself. I suspect she would've sold it, moved to Mexico and lived on the proceeds of the sale. She burned the original ranch house to the ground. Sadie was in the place when she set fire to it.

"Thankfully, Sadie got out. Carla went away,

and we all lived happily ever after."

Aria's lips curled upward. "There. Now was that so painful?"

"Yes," he said.

"Where is Carla now?" Aria asked.

"In jail for attempted murder and arson. I divorced her as soon as I could file the papers."

"And you blame yourself for Carla's transgressions." Aria planted her fists on her hips. "That's ridiculous."

"I should've seen it coming. I knew Carla wasn't right in the head. I just thought she was worried about Sadie."

"You were married to her," Aria said. "You're supposed to trust your spouse. You couldn't have known."

"Yeah, but I should've guessed a lot sooner."

"Maybe you need to do a brain purge like mine. Then you wouldn't still be beating yourself up over something you had no control over." Her lips twisted. "Though I can't say I recommend amnesia for solving your problems. It has some major drawbacks."

Fin nodded toward the runway. "Here they come."

As the lights from the aircraft got closer, the steady thump of rotor blades filled the air.

Moments later, the chopper landed. Hank, Swede and four other men got out and headed toward them.

Swede carried a box. When he reached Fin's truck, Fin dropped the tailgate, and Swede laid the box in the truck bed and opened the top.

Hank stood beside Fin. "We brought some things we might need."

Swede unloaded the box and spread the devices across the truck bed. He pointed to the different groups of electronics. "We have two-way radios and GPS tracking devices. The tracking devices come in several different shapes and sizes."

Hank selected a pretty necklace with a small pendant. "Ari, if you wear this necklace, we can find you." He handed the device to her.

Aria looped it over her head and tucked it inside her shirt.

Hank pulled out another device, smaller than the first that appeared to have tiny teeth. He held it up. "You can use this as a hair clip or just hide it in your hair. It doesn't have quite the range as the pendant, but it's a good backup."

Aria took the clip from Hank, lifted the hair behind her ear, and attached the clip there.

"We could rig you with a radio headset," Swede said. "They're small, like a set of earbuds."

Aria shook her head. "He'll see it. I can't risk making him angrier than he is already. I'd like my sister to remain intact."

"The rest of the team will gear up with the communications equipment," Hank said.

Aria gripped Fin's wrist and turned it so she could see his watch. "I need to be there in ten minutes. It takes that long to get across town. What vehicle am I taking? Or is someone dropping me off a couple of blocks away?"

"I'll take you to within a short walk of the location and follow you in...at a distance." Fin said. "For the record, I don't like this."

"I'll have the tracking devices on me," she said. "If you can't keep up with me, follow the trackers at a distance. And whatever you do, don't let him see you following me."

He nodded. "Let's go."

Aria climbed into the pickup's passenger seat and keyed the location into Fin's cellphone map application.

Fin gave Hank one last glance. "I don't know how this is going down, but I don't like her going in alone."

"We'll be close by," Hank said. "Out of sight, but close enough to assist, if needed."

It would have to be enough. They were out of

time. Fin hurried to climb into the truck, with Aria calling out the directions. They made it to the neighborhood in under ten minutes, giving Aria just enough time to walk the remainder of the distance.

She climbed down out of the truck and met Fin at the front.

He wrapped his arms around her and rested his forehead against hers. "Come back to me," he whispered. "If you do, I'll consider breaking my vow to never fall in love again."

She leaned up on her toes and pressed her lips to his. "Deal."

"We'll get you out."

She met his gaze and nodded. "I'm counting on it." Then she walked away.

Fin had his handgun beneath his jacket, but he'd give anything to have a rifle with a strong scope on it.

He gave Aria a good head start, and then he slipped into the shadows and followed. He couldn't let her out of his sight. Jihadi Jim might be crazy as shit, but he was crafty and dangerous, too.

"Comms check," he said into his headset.

One by one, Hank and his team responded.

At least he had backup. He suspected they'd need it before the night was over.

CHAPTER 10

Aria had memorized the directions from the map and counted the number of streets she had to pass before she turned right, walked another block and turned left. The house was the third on the right.

The neighborhood had seen better days. Some of the homes had been boarded up, others had fallen into disrepair, the roofs sagging and probably taking in water.

When she reached the designated house, her pulse was pounding hard through her veins. Not wanting to risk being late, she marched up to the door and knocked.

No one answered.

She knocked again with the same result.

This time, she gripped the door handle and turned it slowly. It wasn't locked. The hinges creaked as she pushed the door wider, letting some of the glow from the streetlights in.

The room was empty except for an old wooden crate and what appeared to be a pile of rags.

A sheet of paper lay across the wooden crate.

Aria lifted it and carried it into the beam of light shining through the doorway.

The note was written in bold block letters.

REMOVE ALL OF YOUR CLOTHES AND JEWELRY AND LEAVE THEM IN THE CRATE. DRESS IN THE CLOTHING PROVIDED. YOU HAVE TEN MINUTES TO REACH THE NEXT LOCATION. WALK TWO BLOCKS NORTH AND TURN LEFT ON JOHNSON. IN THREE BLOCKS, TURN RIGHT ONTO WILLOW. ENTER THE FIRST ALLEY ON YOUR RIGHT. A WHITE VAN WILL BE WAITING.

Aria's heart raced. Jihadi Jim didn't like to make it easy for his victims.

Without a watch to track the amount of time she had left, she had to hurry and err on the side of being early.

She stripped out of the lovely clothing Sadie had given her, taking off everything, including her bra and panties. She didn't trust the man to let her slide over a minor transgression. Sarah would be terrified as it was. She didn't deserve to be cut up like a side of beef.

The clothes he'd left for her to wear were an old pair of sweats big enough for two of Aria to fit into. She pulled the drawstring on the pants as tight as she could. The shoes were a pair of house slippers that had seen better days.

She removed the necklace Hank had given her with the tracking device inside, but she hesitated to remove the tiny clip hidden in her hair.

Surely, something that small would be overlooked.

She prayed she was right. Her sister's life was at stake.

With the instructions in hand, she left the house, heading north. She didn't dare look around for Fin, Hank and his guys. Following the directions exactly, she arrived at the alley. It was dark, but the white van parked there seemed to glow an eerie blue.

Moving slowly, she approached the van.

When she came abreast of it, the door slid open on the side. A hand reached out and dragged her into the van.

Aria's first instinct was to struggle. She had to fight that instinct. If she fought off the man hauling her into the van, she would only delay getting to Sarah.

Once in the van, the door she'd entered slid closed. As soon as it was completely shut, the door on the opposite side opened. Aria was shoved through it, landing on her feet outside the van.

Two men dressed in black, wearing black face masks, gripped her arms and led her to the rear of an old tank of a Cadillac that had seen better days twenty years before. One man opened the trunk. The other grabbed a black stick from inside the trunk and flipped a switch.

She might have lost her memory for people and places, but Aria knew what the black wand was. They used some just like it to check for tiny electronic devices spies might use to bug buildings.

Would he run it over her head and find the little clip buried in her hair?

She couldn't risk it. Pretending to push her hair behind her ear, she snagged the little clip in her hand and tossed it into the trunk of the Cadillac.

And none too soon. The man touched the wand to each of her ankles, indicating she should spread her legs. She complied and lifted her arms as he moved from her feet to the top of her head.

Her heart beat so fast, she was afraid it would burst inside her chest.

The bug check complete, the man pulled a zip-tie out of his back pocket and secured Aria's wrists in front of her. Then he nodded his head toward the trunk.

A wave of panic struck her as they gripped her arms and propelled her forward. When her thighs hit the back of the car, one of the men gave her a swift shove between the shoulder blades. Aria landed in the trunk, knocking her head at the same spot as when she'd crashed her motorcycle. The guys in black shoved her legs in and slammed the trunk down, cutting off the light and what little air might find its way inside.

She prayed she hadn't just walked into a terrible trap where she'd have no way to escape with her sister.

The only thing that made her feel marginally better was the knowledge Fin was out there with the others. They would've followed her and would continue to follow her until they reached the location where Sarah was being held.

And she'd managed to retain one of the GPS tracking devices. They would be able to follow her as long as she was in the Cadillac. Hampered by the zip-tie securing her wrists, she felt around the trunk for the clip she'd tossed in. When her fingers curled around it, she nearly cried. She quickly tucked it back in her curtain of hair.

She lay in the back of the Cadillac, counting the minutes until she saw her sister. When she did, she hoped she'd remember her face.

The roar of an engine sounded nearby. She assumed the van had left. Splitting up was probably a good idea for the two vehicles.

Seconds later, the Cadillac's engine chugged to life. The vehicle lurched forward and soon was moving faster.

Aria could tell when they went from city streets to the highway. Where were they taking her? Would Fin and Hank be able to follow her tracking device?

Or was she on her own, relying on her ingenuity to get herself and her sister out of the clutches of a madman?

After what felt like an hour and was probably not nearly that long, the vehicle pulled off the highway onto an unimproved road and came to a halt.

Car doors opened and closed. Then the trunk lid opened. The two men who'd shoved her into the trunk pulled her out and loaded her into the back seat of a four-wheel-drive pickup.

Once on the seat, she could push into a sitting position and look out at the terrain.

They were headed up a narrow dirt road with trees overhanging the road low enough that the branches scraped the top of the cab.

Where were they taking her?

And how far behind were Fin and the rest of her backup team?

If they were in the mountains, would the tracking device work? Hadn't Hank said the clip's GPS signal wasn't as strong as the necklace's?

Aria tamped down her rising panic and studied what she could see of the road ahead in the beams of the headlights.

The dirt road leveled out on a hilltop and stopped in front of a log cabin nestled in the trees. If someone wanted to live off the grid, this was the place to do it. You'd have to know where it was to find it.

The truck doors opened. Her escorts dragged her out of the back seat and stood her on her feet. Each man hooked a hand beneath her arms, they walked her to the door of the cabin.

The door opened, and she was escorted through what appeared to be a dated living area with spartan furniture and deer heads mounted on the walls. The only light in the room came from a battery-powered lantern. Anyone walking through the door would assume this was someone's hunting cabin.

She was led to another door hidden in the wall behind a bookshelf filled with a collection of dusty beer mugs. The door opened to a staircase that led down into a basement.

The lighting consisted of one bright bulb dangling from an extension cord. Beneath the light was a single wooden chair with someone slumped over in it.

As Aria moved closer, she gasped. Long dark hair draped the person's face. Even without seeing her dark eyes, Aria knew who it was.

"Sarah?"

The girl's head jerked up, and she strained to look over her shoulder. "Aria!" The next word came out on a sob. "No, no, no. You should've stayed away."

The men led her to a cage that had probably been designed for a large dog breed. It was positioned in front of the spot where Sarah sat with her wrists zip-tied behind the ladder back of the chair, her ankles individually secured to the legs.

The men forced Aria into the cage, locked it with an old padlock, and hung the key on a hook on the wall several feet away from the cell. Well out of reach. With Aria secured, the men climbed the stairs, leaving Aria and Sarah alone.

"Sarah, are you all right?"

Sarah laughed, the tone lacking any mirth. "I'm fine if being stuck in a basement in the middle of who knows where tied to a chair is okay."

"Has he hurt you?"

Her sarcasm faded with a frightened glance toward a table several feet away. "He hasn't hurt me yet. But I think those are his torture tools."

"We're getting out of here, Sarah. Do you hear me?"

Sarah snorted. "How? They lock the door to the basement from the other side. We're tied up, and Mr. Personality is a mean son of a bitch. I doubt he'll just let us walk out of here on our own feet. More likely, we'll go out in a body bag."

Aria studied the basement, searching for a window, a trap door, or anything that would take them directly outside the cabin.

With the light shining brightly overhead, it made the shadows even deeper in the periphery. Aria couldn't see a damned thing.

The door to the basement opened, and footsteps descended the stairs. Because she was surrounded by the bright light above, she couldn't tell who was headed their way until he came to a stop in front of Aria's cage.

He had non-descript brown hair and brown eyes and a look of pure hatred in his eyes.

A blast of cold trepidation washed over Aria. This man had no soul. He was evil to his very core, and nothing Aria could do or say would stop him from doing exactly as he pleased, including brutally torturing his victims.

She had to find a way out and take Sarah with her.

"Don't leave us now, sweetheart," Fin whispered as he stared down at the tracking monitor. It had stopped broadcasting several times over the past twenty minutes. Then it would find a signal minutes later and appear again.

Aria's captors had taken her south of Bozeman on the highway to Big Sky.

Fin and Hank had followed in Fin's truck. Kujo, Swede and two other men—Taz and Chuck—members of Hank's brotherhood, were in Kujo's truck behind Fin.

He figured they weren't much farther than five to ten minutes behind the vehicle with Aria in it.

But five to ten minutes could mean the difference between living and dying.

Fin chose to think positively. The plan from the get-go had been sketchy at best. But with Jihadi Jim's demands and threats, they wouldn't have been able to talk Aria out of going through with it.

They had to trust that they would reach the women in time to keep Jim from executing them in some grizzly fashion.

Fin's gut had been knotted since he'd dropped Aria a couple of blocks from the house on Cherry. She'd emerged from that house, minus the necklace tracker and her clothes.

She'd come out wearing baggy sweats twice as big as she was. She'd carried a sheet of paper as she'd walked several blocks further.

He'd followed her on foot to the next location, with Hank driving the truck a couple of blocks behind him. When he'd seen her get into the white van and the van take off, his heart had sunk to the pit of his belly.

Jihadi Jim was going to make this even more difficult.

Though she was down one of the tracking devices, she still had the small clip. It didn't have as strong a signal, but they were getting enough to follow in the general direction. Hopefully, as they got nearer to it, the signal would be stronger, and they could pinpoint her exact location.

"I didn't have a chance to tell you that Swede got a hit on the facial recognition of one of the men entering the hospital the night Aria was attacked," Hank said.

"Oh, yeah? Who was he?"

"Jimmy Epperson, age twenty-nine, from Des Moines, Iowa."

"Criminal record?" Fin asked.

"A list longer than my arm, from petty theft to assault and battery. There was even a charge of animal cruelty against him."

"A real nice guy." Fin gritted his teeth. "Any siblings?"

Hank nodded. "Joe Epperson, age twenty-seven. He had even more entries on his rap sheet. Jimmy recently returned to the States from Mexico. Swede ran a check and found that he'd flown into Mexico from Turkey the day before he ran Aria off the road."

"Jihadi Jim and Jihadi Joe." Fin snorted. "It's way too cute. They need to be taken down."

"Your Jane Doe nailed one of them."

"And good riddance," Fin said. He liked the sound of *his Jane Doe*. He wouldn't mind it at all if she were his.

"We're coming up on the spot where we lost the signal." Hank pointed to an overgrown dirt road. "That's where we lost it. Pull in."

Fin complied, bumping over deep ruts to make enough room for Kujo's truck to pull off the highway.

"Did you see that?" Hank dug a small flashlight out of his pocket and aimed it toward the brush alongside the rutted dirt road.

Hidden in the underbrush was an ancient Cadillac.

Fin got out of his truck, crossed to the old car and rested his hand on the hood. "It's still warm."

"Then they can't have been gone for long." Hank shined a flashlight on the road then squatted in the dirt. "These are new tire tread marks."

"Looks like we're going on a hike." Fin patted the handgun in the holster beneath his jacket. He'd slipped an extra magazine full of bullets in his pocket. He'd rather be carrying his M4A1 rifle, but he'd make do. A handgun just meant getting closer to the enemy.

Fin took the lead. The team communicated with hand signals and the radio headsets Hank had set them up with.

The climb was steep and long. By the time they

topped a rise and spotted the cabin, they were all sweating and breathing hard.

A couple of men dressed in black stood guard outside the cabin. Each carried an AR15 semi-automatic rifle.

Hank sent Taz with Fin to neutralize the guards. Because Chuck carried a rifle, he was tasked with providing cover for the two men.

With the trees growing close to the cabin, it wasn't hard for Fin and Taz to sneak up on the two men. As deep as the house was in the woods, they probably didn't expect trouble.

Until trouble found them.

Fin took the bigger guy at the same time as Taz handled the other. They held them in a chokehold until they each passed out.

Both men were still alive, so Taz pulled zip-ties and duct tape from a pocket in his cargo pants. The guards were secured and dragged into the woods, away from the cabin. If a bear or wolf happened upon them, Fin wouldn't lose sleep.

The others moved forward and surrounded the cabin.

Fin entered first, his handgun at the ready. Taz and Hank had his six. They moved silently through the cabin but didn't find Aria, Sarah or anyone else for that matter.

They had to be around there somewhere. The guards wouldn't have been out front otherwise.

Fin searched the walls for hidden doors, feeling like time was running out for the women. With a lunatic like Jimmy Epperson calling the shots, they couldn't count on mercy.

CHAPTER 11

THE MAN ARIA assumed was Jihadi Jim crossed to the table lined with an assortment of tools.

"Now that I have your attention, I can fulfill my promise to my dead brother." He looked across to where Aria crouched in the cage. His lips thinned, and his eyes narrowed. "You'll suffer as I have over the suffering and death of a loved one. Joe and I were a team. We did everything together. We played football, went fishing and killed our first deer together." He glared at Aria. "Now he's gone, and I have to carry on our work without him."

He lifted a long rod with an orange handle and carried it over to where Sarah was tied to the chair.

"Leave her alone, you sick son of a bitch. She

didn't kill your brother. I did. If you want your pound of flesh, take it from me."

"I'll get it," Jim said with a smirk. "By making you watch me treat your sister to all of my toys." He touched the end of the stick to Sarah's arm. A sharp buzz sounded, and Sarah yelped, jerking back as much as she could.

He was using a goddamn cattle prod on her.

Aria gripped the cage and shook it. "Leave her alone!"

"And miss the look on your face?" He turned a switch on the device. "Let's up the voltage and see how she likes it."

Aria fought the cage like a wild animal. She lay on her back and kicked the heavy-duty wire again and again as that bastard touched the cattle prod to her sister's leg.

Sarah screamed and tried to pull away, but she couldn't. He kept the device on her leg, sending volts through her, over and over.

Aria rocked the cage and finally managed to turn it over. She landed hard on her side and rolled it again. The welded wire bent but held. She lay on her back and kicked as hard as she could against the door with the padlock. The padlock held tight, but the hinges showed signs of weakening.

After so many shocks, Sarah slumped in her chair, passed out.

With his victim unconscious, Jim turned toward Aria, cattle prod in hand. "Don't you want to feel as good as your sister?"

Aria didn't respond to his level of crazy. She continued to kick at the cage door until one of the hinges broke. Two more steps and Jim would be in range with his cattle prod.

Aria bunched her legs and threw all of her strength into the next kick.

The cage door flew open.

Jim poked the cattle prod through the cage.

The jolt of electricity that charged through her made Aria cry out in pain. She gritted her teeth, grabbed the rod and jammed it through another hole in the wire, trapping the device long enough for her to crawl out of the cage. Once free, she pushed to her feet and swung her bound hands at Jim's head.

He ducked, but not soon enough. Her fists caught him on the side of his head, knocking him backward. He stumbled and fell on his ass.

Aria dove for the torture tools table grabbed the knife and raced over to free her sister's hands.

Jim rolled to his feet and charged the women, hunched down like a bull in the ring.

Aria leaped in front of Sarah, taking the brunt of the hit. She flew backward, her head slamming into the concrete block wall.

Stars swirled around her, and her vision clouded, like smoke closing in on her. She couldn't pass out. Sarah needed her.

She turned to find Jim on the floor behind her, struggling to get to his feet.

Pushing through the haze, Aria rose to her knees, hooked her bound wrists over Jim's head, and pulled back as hard as she could.

The man reached up and clawed at her hands, trying to loosen her hold.

Aria refused to let go

Somehow, Jim lunged to his feet, taking Aria with him, her hold slipping only a moment before she applied renewed force.

Jim staggered backward and rammed her into the wall with enough force to knock the air from her lungs.

Her hold weakened long enough for Jim to grip her arms and duck beneath them.

Unable to draw air into her lungs, Aria leaned her back against the wall and willed herself to remain calm.

Unable to move, Aria could only watch as Jim spun, scooped a battery-powered drill from the tools now scattered across the floor, and lunged toward her with a sharp drill bit spinning.

He almost reached her when Sarah leaped at him from the side, swinging the wooden chair she'd been trapped in moments before.

The chair crashed over Jim's head and sent him flying across the floor to crash into the edge of the metal cage. Blood ran from his hairline into his eyes.

His face turned a mottled red. He grabbed a machete, lurched to his feet and came at them again.

With nothing to defend them from the crazed man, Sarah and Aria ran for the stairs.

As Sarah began climbing, the machete sailed past Aria's head, bounced off the concrete block wall, and dropped beside her feet. She scooped up the massive blade and turned to defend herself and her sister.

In a blinding rage, Jihadi Jim rushed her.

Aria was shoved to the side at the last second.

Fin ducked low and met the force of Jim's attack. He staggered backward and bumped into Aria.

While Fin teetered and tried to right himself, Jim wrenched the machete from Aria's hands.

He raised the weapon high above his head.

A shot rang out.

For a moment, all motion ceased.

Then the machete slipped from Jihadi Jim's hands and fell to the floor. Jim clutched his chest, his eyes wide, and then dropped where he stood, hitting the ground with a loud thud.

Aria's gaze went to Fin as he held his weapon still aimed at Jim.

"I don't think he's getting up," Aria said.

She pushed the barrel of Fin's weapon to the side and stepped into his arms. "Are you going to make a habit of rescuing me? That's three for three."

He looped his arm around her waist and pulled her to him. "For a chance at a kiss, I'll rescue you every chance I get. You're my Jane Doe, and I'm breaking my vow to never fall in love again. I might as well. I'm already halfway in love with you. Does that scare you?"

She laughed. "Machetes and cattle prods scare me. You falling in love with me...terrifies me. What if I get my memory back, and you discover I'm a horrible raving bitch? I'd lose you forever."

He chuckled and kissed her hard. "I'll take my chances. I think I started falling in love with you when I saw you ride your motorcycle straight into the path of that machine gunner."

"Wait...what?" Sarah appeared beside Aria. "You rode a motorcycle toward a live machine gun?" Sarah shook her head. "Will you stop it already?" Her eyes filled with tears. "You're the only family I have left. What would I do if I lost you?" She wrapped her arms around Aria and hugged her so tightly, Aria could barely breathe.

"I'm not going anywhere, baby girl. And my motorcycle riding days are done."

"And the machine guns?" Sarah leaned back and pinned Aria with a pointed glance.

"Those, too." Aria didn't quite remember her sister, but the hug felt familiar. Her past would come back, eventually. She just had to give it time.

She met Fin's gaze and smiled. Her present was pretty awesome. And her future held a whole lot of promise.

EPILOGUE

"Fin, can you bring Emma and Mac inside?" Sadie called out. "It's bath time."

"Coming." Fin, holding baby McClain in one arm, held the door for Aria and Emma. The two had become fast friends and loved brushing each other's hair. Aria loved Emma's silky blond tresses, and Aria's dark, thick mane entranced Emma.

"Emma, go get your pajamas out of your dresser and bring them in the bathroom," Sadie said.

"Miss Aria, will you help me?" Emma looked up at Aria with her big blue eyes. "Please?"

Fin almost laughed out loud at how easily Emma conned Aria into doing things for her.

Hell, she did it to him, too. He couldn't resist her puppy dog eyes any more than Aria.

"I'd love to." Aria followed the little girl down the hallway into her bedroom.

"Mac and Emma are going to miss their Uncle Fin." Sadie took Mac from Fin's arm and kissed his forehead. "Isn't that right, little man?"

"I'm going to miss changing his poopy diapers…." Fin gave his sister a wicked grin, "said no one ever."

"You have to admit it was good practice," Sadie called over her shoulder. "One of these days, you'll have little ones to love on." She shot him a stern look. "Don't wait too long, though. I want our children to grow up together. Nothing's better than growing up with your cousins on a ranch. This brings us back to the big question… When are you going to come home for good?"

"You know I have a commitment to Uncle Sam for another year." His smile spread across his face. "But after that, I'm heading home. I hadn't realized how much I missed this ranch and the Crazy Mountains until I came home."

"I'm glad you finally came to your senses," Sadie leaned up and kissed her brother's cheek. "It isn't the same without my brother."

"Shoot, you have Hank and a dozen other brothers to keep you company. You don't need me."

Sadie smiled happily. "You're right. I love all the brothers of the Brotherhood Protectors and their ladies. We're one big, happy, messy family. But you and I grew up together, Fin. You'll always have a special place in my heart."

"And you in mine, sis. I shouldn't have stayed gone so long." He kissed the top of her shiny gold hair and dropped a kiss on Mac's head as well.

The baby giggled and swatted at him.

"Well, one thing's for sure, Hank wants you on the team. You showed him you have what it takes to be a member of the Brotherhood."

"I only did what was right."

"And that's what makes you fit in. These men are strong, courageous and have a solid moral compass. They don't get better than that."

"Are you still trying to talk Fin into joining the team?" Hank appeared in the doorway of Mac's room.

"Damn right, I am. All for purely selfish reasons. I want him home." Sadie handed Mac to Hank. "He needs a bath."

"Are you trying to tell me something?" Hank cocked an eyebrow.

Sadie did the same and upped the ante by crossing her arms over her chest.

Hank laughed. "I hear you loud and clear." He

turned with Mac. "Come on, bud, we have some water to splash."

Sadie smiled as Hank left with Mac. "Hank's a good father."

"I can see that. The kids love him."

His sister poked a finger in his chest. "When are you going get back out there and find that someone special?"

"Who says I haven't?" He gave Sadie a sly grin.

Aria chose that moment to appear in the hallway with Emma. Her smile lit his world and made it a brighter place than he'd ever known.

"You've only known each other less than two weeks," Sadie said quietly. "How can you be sure?"

"I knew Carla all my life, yet I really didn't know her." His heart swelled at the sight of Aria bending to talk to Emma on her level. "I didn't even know Aria's name, and I fell in love with her anyway." He held up his hand. "Don't worry. We're going to take it slow. I owe the Army another year, and she wants to spend that time figuring out what she wants to do now that she's not working for the State Department. That'll also give her time to regain her memories."

"Or not," Sadie added.

"Then it will give her time to accept it and make new ones. In the meantime, it'll be a long-distance relationship, with a lot of going back and forth while she settles her father's estate."

"Sounds like you have a plan." Sadie hugged him around the middle. "I'm happy for you. And if Aria is badass enough to put up with you, that counts for a lot."

"I'm glad I have your approval." Fin's grin broadened. "Now, if you'll excuse me, I have some kissing to catch up on before I ship out tomorrow." He strode toward Aria, who straightened and gave him a blinding smile.

Aria had lost her past, and he had let go of his. As he pulled her into his arms, he knew in his heart they'd found their present and future together.

SEAL SALVATION

BROTHERHOOD PROTECTORS COLORADO
BOOK #1

New York Times & *USA Today*
Bestselling Author

ELLE JAMES

SEAL SALVATION

BROTHERHOOD PROTECTORS
Colorado

New York Times & USA Today Bestselling Author

ELLE JAMES

HANK PATTERSON PACED the length of the confer-ence table in the basement of his home in Montana, muttering, "No man left behind."

"Hey, boss." Axel Svenson, the giant of a Viking, ducked as he descended the steps into the head-quarters of one of the finest security firms in the state of Montana.

Hank, a former Navy SEAL, had started the Brotherhood Protectors after he'd rescued movie star Sadie McClain when her bodyguards were less than effective. Since then, he'd married the movie star, had a couple of kids and hired a number of former Army, Navy and Marine special operations, highly-trained operatives, to provide security or conduct dangerous missions where the govern-ment wasn't or couldn't get involved.

He took pride in the fact he'd helped so many of his military brotherhood find a place to fit into the civilian world.

With a large contingent of his men based in Montana, he needed to create other bases of operations. He'd set up an office in Hawaii, where former SEAL Jace "Hawk" Hawkins was the only man currently handling business there. He and some of his men had discussed other locations, including Washington, DC, New Orleans, Atlanta, New York City and Colorado.

Having grown up on a ranch, Hank liked the idea of setting up another location in an area much like his beloved Montana. Now, all he needed was to find the men to run the location.

"Hey, Hank," a familiar voice sounded from the staircase. "What's up?"

Hank lifted his chin toward Joseph "Kujo" Kuntz. "Sorry to take you away from your family on a Sunday."

Kujo descended the stairs, followed by his retired Military Working Dog, Six. "No problem. Molly had to go to her office in Bozeman to pick up some files and check in with her supervisor."

Hank smiled. "How's the pregnancy going?"

Kujo shoved a hand through his hair. "First

three months were a bitch with morning sickness, but she's feeling good now."

"Will she continue to work for the FBI after the baby is born?" Hank asked.

Kujo's lips twisted, and his brow dipped. "Much as I'd like her to quit and raise our baby, it wouldn't be fair to ask her to do that. She's good at her job."

"And you and Six are good at yours." Hank's brow rose. "You're not considering quitting, are you?"

Kujo laughed. "No way. But we're in the process of interviewing nannies."

Hank nodded. "Glad to hear it. You're a vital member of the team, here."

"Thanks," Kujo said. "I'm sure you didn't invite me here to ask about morning sickness and babies. You've got your hands full with your own children, one of which is a newborn, probably keeping you awake at night."

"Truth." Hank's smile slipped. "Think you can get away for a couple weeks before the baby is born?"

Kujo nodded slowly. "Where did you have in mind?"

Hank nodded his head toward the white board

on the wall where a computer image of a state was projected. "I've got a lead on a location for our new office."

Kujo stepped closer. "New office? Where?"

"Your old stomping grounds," Hank said. "Colorado."

A grin spread across Kujo's face. "That's great." As soon as the grin came it faded. "Only, I can't be gone for long with Molly being pregnant."

Hank nodded. "I don't want you to move out there permanently. I just need you to get out there, set up shop and hire a few good men, keeping in mind that one of them will head up the location."

"I hate to be gone so long from Molly," Kujo said. "If it's okay with her, I can give you a few weeks. She's only four months along, which gives me a little time that I can be away."

"I wanted to be with Sadie every day of her pregnancy," Hank said.

"I'd like to be with Molly every day of hers. But if you need me to go to Colorado, now would be better than later this year."

Hank nodded. "Good. And I have someone in mind for leading the new team out there." His brow wrinkled. "Only he's a work in progress."

Kujo frowned. "What do you mean...work in progress?"

Hank sighed. "Not only has he lost a leg, he's lost his way."

Kujo's eyes narrowed. "I can understand. I was at my lowest when you offered me a job. If it hadn't been for you and the Brotherhood Protectors..." Kujo shook his head, his hand going automatically to Six's head.

The dog nuzzled his fingers, sensing his handler's emotions.

"I figured you of all people would see where I'm going with this. And you're from Colorado. You'll appreciate going back."

Kujo ran a hand over Six's smooth, sable head. "You saved my life, and Six's, not long ago," Kujo said quietly.

"You and Six were worth saving. And so is Jake Cogburn."

Kujo's eyes widened. "Jake 'The Cog' Cogburn?"

Hank nodded again. "He's in a bad way, from what I hear."

"Like I was when you found me and made me rescue Six?"

"Exactly. I figured you'd have a better connection with the SEAL."

Kujo drew in a deep breath. "He has to be ready to make the change."

Hank laughed. "And you were?"

Kujo grinned. "I wasn't. But you were convincing. And knowing Six would be euthanized if I didn't go to him, motivated me."

"Cog needs someone to motivate him," Hank said. "He needs a purpose. He needs to know he's still relevant in this world."

"And you think I'm the man to pull him up by his bootstraps?" Kujo shook his head. "I don't know. Might take more than the few weeks I can give to the job."

Hank clapped Kujo on the back. "I've seen your work. I know you can handle it."

"And you want me to set up a new office for the Brotherhood Protectors?" Kujo shook his head. "That, in itself, will take some time. I'll have to find a building to rent or purchase and equip it with all the infrastructure needed." He waved his hand at Hank's basement. "This takes time."

"I have a connection near Colorado Springs." Hank turned and walked away. "He's a former Marine gunnery sergeant running a dude ranch near a small town called Fool's Gold, which is located outside of Colorado Springs." He touched several keys on a computer keyboard, and an image popped up on a screen.

Kujo looked over Hank's shoulder to view a map on the monitor.

"I think Gunny Tate's ranch has everything we need to set up shop. Great location, private enough and they need the money we'd pay in rent. It's a win-win situation. Besides, the ranch will give us the cover we need to run our operations without detection."

"Kind of like what you have here." Kujo nodded. "We're just a bunch of ranch hands, until we're given an assignment."

"Exactly." Hank's grin widened. "Gunny Tate is a character. He raised his only child singlehandedly after his wife died in childbirth. I believe that child is grown now and working the dude ranch with him. Gunny is a blustery curmudgeon with a heart of gold. Met him at McP's a million years ago after BUD/S training. His team was celebrating his transfer to a recruiting command in Colorado. He's been in Colorado ever since."

"Recruiting command?" Kujo's brows rose. "Who'd he piss off?"

Hank shook his head. "He opted to go into recruiting to end his career in a place of his choice. Being a single father raising a child, when he could be deployed at a moment's notice, wore on him. He wanted to slow down and give the child a steady home to grow up in."

"Boy or girl?" Kujo asked.

Hank grinned. "Name's Rucker. Trust Gunny to give him a tough name. I can only assume he's a boy. I never had the pleasure of meeting him."

Kujo drew in a deep breath, let it out and clapped his hands together. "When do you want me to go? This week? Next week? You name it."

Hank picked up a sheet of paper off the printer beside the monitor. "Your plane leaves at six in the morning from Bozeman and arrives in Colorado Springs before noon. That should give you plenty of time to find the town of Fool's Gold and Lost Valley Ranch. Gunny is expecting you and will take you to where Cogburn is holed up."

Kujo leaned his head toward the German Shepherd lying patiently at his feet. "What about Six?"

Hank smiled. "If you want, I can book him in the seat beside yours on the airplane."

Kujo glanced down at Six. "Guess I'm going home to Colorado. I'd like Six to stay here with Molly."

Six rose to his feet. Ready to go.

"Sorry, boy," Kujo said. "You're needed here."

Hank held out his hand. "Good luck convincing Cog we have a place for him. He was a helluva SEAL and a leader among his team. If you can pull him out of his funk, he'll make a great team leader for our Colorado location. That is, unless you'd like to take that position…?" Hank raised his eyebrows.

Kujo shook his head. "Molly's established herself at the Bozeman office of the FBI. They know her and what she's capable of. With her being pregnant, it would be a bad time to move. She'd have to start all over making her mark."

Hank nodded. "Figured as much. Besides, she has a great support system here to take care of your baby when you're both called to duty."

"Exactly. I wouldn't ask her to move now. Maybe in a year or two, but not now. I do miss Colorado. Fortunately, Montana is a lot like where I came from. Wide open spaces, blue sky, mountains and more. Here, I have a team I love working with." He shook Hank's hand. "Thanks for pulling me back into the land of the living."

"You're welcome. Now go get Cog. I have a feeling he'll be just the right fit for running the Colorado office of the Brotherhood Protectors."

As Kujo and Six left the basement conference room, Hank's gaze followed. If anyone could get Jake Cogburn to pull his head out of his ass and get to work, Kujo was the one.

"Hank?" Sadie's voice sounded from the top of the stairs.

"Yeah, babe," he responded, taking the stairs two at a time.

His beautiful wife stood with baby Mac cradled in her arms.

Hank leaned close and captured her mouth with his. "What's up, beautiful?"

She kissed him back and smiled up at him. "Is Kujo going to Colorado?"

Hank nodded. "He is."

Sadie nodded. "I'm glad. If I didn't have to show up on the set of my next film, you could go." She frowned. "I could call and reschedule."

"Don't. Kujo can handle Cog." He kissed Sadie again. "Besides, I'm looking forward to having Mac and Emma all to myself while I miss their mama."

Sadie's smile spread across her face. "I love you, Hank Patterson. And I love that you care about your former teammates enough to help them out."

He leaned back, raising his eyebrows. "Are you kidding? They're helping me. I couldn't have built this business so big and so fast without them."

Hank took Mac from Sadie's arms and carried him into the living room where Emma played with her collection of stuffed animals spread out across the area rug.

He prayed Cogburn wouldn't send Kujo packing. The man really needed a purpose for his life. If he had that, he'd realize that being short a leg wasn't the end of the world.

ABOUT THE AUTHOR

ELLE JAMES also writing as MYLA JACKSON is a *New York Times* and *USA Today* Bestselling author of books including cowboys, intrigues and paranormal adventures that keep her readers on the edges of their seats. When she's not at her computer, she's traveling, snow skiing, boating, or riding her ATV, dreaming up new stories. Learn more about Elle James at www.ellejames.com

Website | Facebook | Twitter | GoodReads | Newsletter | BookBub | Amazon

Or visit her alter ego Myla Jackson at mylajackson.com
Website | Facebook | Twitter | Newsletter

Follow Me!
www.ellejames.com
ellejamesauthor@gmail.com

Breaking Dawn (#8)

Breaking Promises (#9)

Iron Horse Legacy

Soldier's Duty (#1)

Ranger's Baby (#2)

Marine's Promise (#3)

SEAL's Vow (#4)

Warrior's Resolve (#5)

Brotherhood Protectors Series

Montana SEAL (#1)

Bride Protector SEAL (#2)

Montana D-Force (#3)

Cowboy D-Force (#4)

Montana Ranger (#5)

Montana Dog Soldier (#6)

Montana SEAL Daddy (#7)

Montana Ranger's Wedding Vow (#8)

Montana SEAL Undercover Daddy (#9)

Cape Cod SEAL Rescue (#10)

Montana SEAL Friendly Fire (#11)

Montana SEAL's Mail-Order Bride (#12)

SEAL Justice (#13)

Ranger Creed (#14)

Delta Force Rescue (#15)

Dog Days of Christmas (#16)

Montana Rescue (#17)

Montana Ranger Returns (#18)

Hot SEAL Salty Dog (SEALs in Paradise)

Hot SEAL, Hawaiian Nights (SEALs in Paradise)

Hot SEAL Bachelor Party (SEALs in Paradise)

Hot SEAL, Independence Day (SEALs in Paradise)

Brotherhood Protectors Vol 1

The Outrider Series

Homicide at Whiskey Gulch (#1)

Hideout at Whiskey Gulch (#2)

Held Hostage at Whiskey Gulch (#3)

Setup at Whiskey Gulch (#4)

Hellfire Series

Hellfire, Texas (#1)

Justice Burning (#2)

Smoldering Desire (#3)

Hellfire in High Heels (#4)

Playing With Fire (#5)

Up in Flames (#6)

Total Meltdown (#7)

Declan's Defenders

Marine Force Recon (#1)

Show of Force (#2)

Full Force (#3)

Driving Force (#4)

Tactical Force (#5)

Disruptive Force (#6)

Mission: Six

One Intrepid SEAL

Two Dauntless Hearts

Three Courageous Words

Four Relentless Days

Five Ways to Surrender

Six Minutes to Midnight

Hearts & Heroes Series

Wyatt's War (#1)

Mack's Witness (#2)

Ronin's Return (#3)

Sam's Surrender (#4)

The Billionaire Glitch Date (#6)

The Billionaire Perfect Date (#7) coming soon

The Billionaire Replacement Date (#8) coming soon

The Billionaire Wedding Date (#9) coming soon

Ballistic Cowboy

Hot Combat (#1)

Hot Target (#2)

Hot Zone (#3)

Hot Velocity (#4)

Cajun Magic Mystery Series

Voodoo on the Bayou (#1)

Voodoo for Two (#2)

Deja Voodoo (#3)

Cajun Magic Mysteries Books 1-3

SEAL Of My Own

Navy SEAL Survival

Navy SEAL Captive

Navy SEAL To Die For

Navy SEAL Six Pack

Devil's Shroud Series

Deadly Reckoning (#1)

Deadly Engagement (#2)

Deadly Liaisons (#3)

Deadly Allure (#4)

Deadly Obsession (#5)

Deadly Fall (#6)

Covert Cowboys Inc Series

Triggered (#1)

Taking Aim (#2)

Bodyguard Under Fire (#3)

Cowboy Resurrected (#4)

Navy SEAL Justice (#5)

Navy SEAL Newlywed (#6)

High Country Hideout (#7)

Clandestine Christmas (#8)

Thunder Horse Series

Hostage to Thunder Horse (#1)

Thunder Horse Heritage (#2)

Thunder Horse Redemption (#3)

Christmas at Thunder Horse Ranch (#4)

Demon Series

Hot Demon Nights (#1)

Demon's Embrace (#2)

Tempting the Demon (#3)

Lords of the Underworld

Witch's Initiation (#1)

Witch's Seduction (#2)

The Witch's Desire (#3)

Possessing the Witch (#4)

Stealth Operations Specialists (SOS)

Nick of Time

Alaskan Fantasy

Boys Behaving Badly Anthology

Rogues (#1)

Blue Collar (#2)

Pirates (#3)

Stranded (#4)

First Responder (#5)

Blown Away

Warrior's Conquest

Enslaved by the Viking Short Story

Conquests

Smokin' Hot Firemen

Protecting the Colton Bride

Protecting the Colton Bride & Colton's Cowboy Code

Heir to Murder

Secret Service Rescue

High Octane Heroes

Haunted

Engaged with the Boss

Cowboy Brigade

Time Raiders: The Whisper

Bundle of Trouble

Killer Body

Operation XOXO

An Unexpected Clue

Baby Bling

Under Suspicion, With Child

Texas-Size Secrets

Cowboy Sanctuary

Lakota Baby

Dakota Meltdown

Beneath the Texas Moon

Printed in Great Britain
by Amazon

81954969R00142